"These stories are perfect gems: polished for clarity, cut with precision by an expert hand so that they throw off light and color. Czyzniejewski is a funny, smart writer, crafting characters and situations with abundant wit and heart. A brilliant and entertaining collection—and one I'll be returning to again and again."

—Charles Yu, author of *How to Live Safely in a Science Fictional Universe*

"With their blunt but tender sense of humor, the stories in this collection very poignantly redraw the lines, or our perception of the lines, of intimacy, public versus private space, connection, the self. They pull back layer after layer of fallacy, the fantasy, the glamour, the romance of the world of love. They remind us that we live in a world not of love or not-love, but a world of people who, despite their public calm and collectedness, are brimming over with a beautiful messiness not so far from the surface of things, and it is the messiness that makes us interesting, that endears us to each other, that keeps us exploring and reinventing ourselves and jockeying for position within a world that is, ultimately, no less messy or confused."

—*Heavy Feather Review*

### Praise for *Chicago Stories: 40 Dramatic Fictions*

"Chicago, a page at a time. Michael Czyzniejewski gets right to the point in telling the city's stories."

—*Chicago Tribune*

"Flexing impressive literary chops, the beer vendor/creative-writing professor captures both the tough, defensive exterior and the vulnerable, often-broken heart of his city."

—*Time Out Chicago*

# I WILL LOVE YOU
# FOR THE REST
# OF MY LIFE

### BREAKUP STORIES

## MICHAEL
## CZYZNIEJEWSKI

CURBSIDE SPLENDOR PUBLISHING

The stories contained herein are works of fiction. All incidents, situations, institutions, governments, and people are fictional and any similarity to characters or persons living or dead is strictly coincidental.

Published by Curbside Splendor Publishing, Inc., Chicago, Illinois, in 2015.

First Edition
Copyright © 2015 by Michael Czyzniejewski
Library of Congress Control Number: 2014953061

ISBN 978-1-94-043028-7
Edited by Peter Jurmu
Designed by Alban Fischer
Cover art by Ryan Bradley
Manufactured in the United States of America.

www.curbsidesplendor.com

# CONTENTS

*For Karen,*
*who didn't inspire a single word of this book.*

I WILL LOVE YOU
FOR THE REST OF MY LIFE

# A CHANGE OF HEART

It was my turn to sell something of value to me. Manny had hocked his stereo the previous week, and our utilities were due, final notices stacked in heaping piles. Manny examined my earrings and keys to an unstartable car, but a flash of light reflecting off my engagement ring caught my eye, as Manny himself had years before. I slipped it off and leaned over to kiss his lips, screwing the diamond into his palm, closing his fingers tight. Soon, Manny ran off, saddened, but making promises of gas, electricity, and maybe, if enough was left over, cheap wine.

Hours later, Manny returned to our white apartment, not with stamped receipts or even magic beans, but a box, white and decorated with colored designs: tiny hearts, purple and red, a valentine in December. Through the cellophane window I spied another heart, this one not cartoonish—two bumps slipping to a point—but artificial: medical, plastic, shaped like the thumb side of a closed fist. "Go ahead and open it," Manny said, skimming through kitchen drawers, "but then hop in the shower and scrub down." I kept the package sealed, scratching at the cellophane, but soon stepped into the tub, keeping the curtain half drawn, the door locked, waiting for cold droplets to fall hot.

Merlot, two bottles dripping with cooler condensation, lay between Manny's legs on the living room floor, centering a box-shaped groove where a TV once sat, facing a sectional that had split long ago. A towel with my embroidered initials was wrapped around my head, the rest of me cold and dripping like the magnums collapsed against Manny's thighs. Manny instructed me to spread the towel across the blue card table in the kitchen, cleared of bills, beer cans, and bottles, wiped clean with a damp cloth from the sink, water streaks like tigers' stripes, dried and obvious in certain light. I did not like the look of the blade Manny ran across his rubber-gloved palms, but when he began peeling wrappers and unscrewing corks, I was his.

Waking some time later, in dim lamplight, I wanted my engagement ring back, feeling its absence against my finger. Examining myself further, I found a scar stretching from navel to throat, dissecting my breasts, my scarred skin sewn shut with a rainbow of threads: navy, yellows, reds. A sleeping bag wrapped Manny, out on the floor next to our bed. One twist of my shoulders opened his eyes. "We can get the liver next week," he said sweetly, his left eye fluttering open and shut, "if I go back with mine." He brought his hand up to my forehead, stroking it back through my hair, his gold wedding ring rolling against my scalp. The fluorescent light fixture fizzled, leaving us together still, in the dark.

# ALL OUT

My sister once saw Meryl Streep naked in a public shower. It was 1980 and they were somewhere near Virginia Beach. Meryl Streep was already famous, just not yet Meryl Streep. Stacey, my sister, was pulling the top of her swimsuit over her head when Meryl Streep and another woman came in. Stacey said Meryl Streep made definitive eye contact, first with her nipples, then her eyes. Meryl Streep then stripped, enjoying her casual nudity, somehow both lithe and supple, not a trace of shame. Stacey watched as she and her friend helped each other into their swimsuits, not erotically, more like actors backstage readying for a scene. After an ample application of suntan lotion, Meryl Streep's friend looked at Stacey, her swimsuit long on and her boyfriend waiting outside, and asked her how warm the water was in Virginia that time of year. Stacey said, "Real warm," and Meryl Streep said, "Fantastic!" and that was the last time until a nipple flash in *Silkwood* that Stacey saw Meryl Streep naked.

My mailman has a pink heart-surgery scar bifurcating his chest. I see it on hot days, his baby blue unbuttoned, the front walk visible from my side window. Cody is taut and tan, and how a man that fit needed open heart, I don't know. When I could still ride the Go-Go, I'd wait on the porch for the only human contact I'd get all day. "Looking sweet, Mirabelle," Cody would say, or "What's cookin', good lookin'?" handing me whatever. I'd watch him walk away, down the street, the whole way back to his truck. I imagined his hands on me, callused with nimble fingers, so good at sorting, and while I entertained few illusions, I could picture it and still do. It's the scar that makes it possible, believable, surgery like that for someone so unlikely. I've applied a narrative to Cody: a husky kid, a chunky teen, obese adult, heart attack at twenty-six, and voilà, the scar. With diet and exercise, he's a third his peak weight, but he'll never forget. He'd know me. Empathize. Walk me down his path. I have my sisters give Cody a hundred dollars and a bottle of brandy every Christmas. It's not bribery, but maybe it helps keep him on my route.

Candace, my other sister, spent a part of her life working as a pornography actress. Nobody in our family knows but me, not even Stacey, and I only know because I recognized her in a movie. We thought Candace was in Kyrgyzstan with the Peace Corps, searching for land mines, but really, she was in Stuttgart, building a career and fan base in porn. After two years, Candace returned, told us a couple of stories about little villagers with no legs, but I knew better and told her I knew. I had a tape, one that involved four men and another woman, an obese woman, nothing like me, but enough to imply the connection. I promised I wouldn't tell our parents, still alive and proud as pumpkins, but only if she told me all about it. Candace denied everything so I scooted toward my door, yelling, "Mom, guess what?" and Candace grabbed my cart, relenting. She made me wait until our parents were at church, and even then, she whispered everything. It started with dancing, which Candace studied in college, moved to dancing with girls, some photos with men, and then she was too far in so she went all out. She told me about her last movie, set in a soccer stadium, where she'd entertained two teams of guys, all of them lined up to take their turn. That's when she was done; it was her line and she'd crossed it. In the end, she'd saved $48,000 and somehow was spared any lasting infection. The only detail she refused to share concerned the movie I'd seen her in, with the large lady, and when I pressed, she left the house. I didn't see her for two months. When she came for Easter brunch, I handed her an egg I'd dyed purple, her name in white crayon script. That got us talking, but never again about her acting.

My first and only sexual experience to date was, more or less, a tick bath. Last May, some kid threw a rock through the window behind my bed, the one flush against the evergreens, and nobody stopped by to fix it for a week. The next morning, I counted five black dots inset in my skin, a dozen more the day after. Candace was coming once a week to play rummy, but by her day, I was more tick than woman. Candace called Stacey and Stacey arranged for my bather, Zoe, to visit ASAP, chiding me for not calling her right away: "You're covered in ticks, Maribelle, Jesus." Zoe arrived soon after. I liked Zoe and never considered her in any physical way, yet as she tweezed the ticks, she never flinched and never judged. By bath time, I'd noticed her Cody-tan, how her ponytail and small breasts bobbed in unison, that nothing ever got her down. As she rubbed in antibacterial lotion, I lost my breath, and as she worked my thighs, I felt something inside connect my knees and elbows, not like electricity, not like a seizure. I rotated my head a few inches to the left, let out a tiny sound, like a cat acknowledging a large dog, and pointed my toes at zero-degree angles. Zoe asked if I was OK and I told her I was happy she'd come on short notice, that I'd make sure my sisters paid her double. She said it wasn't necessary, that it was her pleasure, but I insisted, "No, no. It was all mine."

Back when I was still walking, my sisters attempted matchmaking. The first guy was the janitor from Stacey's gym, a man twice my age who didn't know he was on a blind date. When Stacey brought him inside, he asked which rooms he'd be in charge of and if we had our own rug scrubber. After him came the priest recently excommunicated from our parents' church, also twice as old as me, a trend I would not dignify by emerging from my room. Candace's accountant was next, and he was the best of the lot, but as it turned out, had not always been a man, which I didn't judge him for, though on our first date, he told me not to get attached, as he was changing his mind again. Their final attempt tipped the scales. The whole week leading up to the date, both Stacey and Candace talked a lot about companionship, using that word, "companionship," like it was the secret word of the day. "What I like about my relationship with Jasper is the *companionship*," Stacey said, as if Jasper were a ficus and didn't look like Kevin Costner in *Tin Cup*. When this last candidate came to pick me up, I recognized him as the high school band director, the man who got our priest excommunicated. The companionship angle suddenly made sense, but I declined, anyway. That was eleven years ago, the last and closest thing to a chance I've ever had.

Stacey calls this morning to tell me she's adopting a three-legged monkey. Stacey's a pediatrician who spends a month each year working at an orphanage in the Philippines. She found a monkey, she explains, with three legs, and is working on papers to bring it home, to make it her pet. I can't decide what kind of limbs a three-legged monkey has. Is Stacey counting the front paws as legs, meaning this monkey has three limbs total, one limb lost? Or does she mean this monkey has two front paws and three legs in the back, five total? I want to believe in the five-limbed version, the super-monkey. Can a five-limbed monkey climb trees faster? Open green bananas? Play soccer? Before I can ask, my sister says she's forgotten to deposit money in my account and will have Candace or Zoe run to the bank then drop by, maybe play some cards. Stacey says she needs to go—malaria is everywhere and these Filipino kids are a naked mosquito buffet—and that makes me think of Meryl Streep. I ask, "Stacey, do you remember seeing Meryl Streep undress?" Stacey laughs, says she hasn't thought of that in years, not even when she sees Streep films. "I watched *Julie & Julia* on the plane and her tits never crossed my mind." I wonder at that, seeing a celebrity naked, full frontal, then forgetting. I wonder if Zoe forgets me. I picture Zoe telling her husband, her friends, describing me, going into detail. I hope she is kind. Stacey says good-bye, but before she hangs up, I use my most definitive voice, pushing deep from my diaphragm, just to let my sister know I am as serious as I can make myself: "Stacey, I want that monkey."

# WE WERE YOUNG

Cross-country by train, Bangor, Maine, to San Diego. We had time to talk. We were trying to figure us out, if we should commit. My logic: 3,200 miles in a train compartment, 3,200 miles back, we could pay a mortgage, raise kids, survive affairs. She wanted to see Mexico.

"What's the worst thing you've ever done?" she asked. It was the first thing she'd said since Chicago. We were in the plains.

"Like to a woman?"

"Overall," she said. "But if that's what popped into your mind."

Everything I remembered involved women. I couldn't tell her the worst thing, unsure if I could speak it aloud.

"It's not interesting," I said.

"Let's hear it."

"I embarrassed a girl."

"Sexually?" Her fist tensed, her knuckles gliding up my thigh.

"No." I should have made something up. "I humiliated her."

"Non-sexually?"

"It was her birthday. She was young. All her friends saw."

"What did you do?"

It was too late.

"Do you remember Charco Snaps?"

"Excuse me?"

8

"Charco Snaps. Little square doggie biscuits, black, like charcoal. My dog inhaled them."

"Did she have a fetish or something? The girl, I mean."

"She ate some as a kid."

"Some?"

"A whole box."

"Who cares what anyone does when they're kids?"

"Exactly," I said, but didn't necessarily agree. "But she shared her secret with me."

"Why?"

"We were doing what you and I are doing now, exploring each other."

She smiled like she knew something. "Were you in bed?"

"Maybe." We were.

"She sounds lovely," she said. "Did she have ticks, too? Ringworm?"

Outside our window, the sky looked dark. I realized, after staring, the dark was the mountains, the Rockies. They ate the sky.

"We talked in bed a lot. Being in bed meant something to her. I was her first—I think. In between, we'd talk. Tell stories. Make lists."

"Like for groceries?"

"No, things we liked." I'd tried the same with this woman early on and she wouldn't have it. I wondered if she was remembering this now. "Favorite albums. Favorite movies. Ice cream flavors. Condiments."

"You were in love," she said.

"Maybe. I was young. When you're nineteen and a pretty girl, of her own free will, likes to . . . ."

"You were a virgin, too, huh?"

"No," I said. I wasn't, but barely. "We hit it off. We both liked the Gin Blossoms and veal parmesan and *Groundhog Day*. We hung around. She met my idiot roommates and didn't run. I met her friends, who were ghastly but manageable. We scheduled classes together for the next term. We started thinking about summer. She was from Oregon.

"Her birthday was right after Thanksgiving. We'd had a pregnancy scare—she was late, then there it was, a beautiful red dot on her underwear. Things were tense. I was flying to Portland the day after Christmas and we thought we were going to have to tell them about a baby."

My story was interrupted: lavatory break. She told me to hold my place, how she wanted to hear the rest. This wasn't where she'd wanted this to go. I was all love letters and she wanted to know who I'd fucked over. The break lasted a while, but she asked me to finish when she returned.

"So right before finals, it's her twentieth birthday and I plan a surprise party. I track down her friends, get her roommates to take her out so I can decorate. Dozens of people show up. Her sister drives down from Daytona. My roommates, wanting to scam on her roommates, come, too, and bring Jell-O shots. People are drunk and happy."

"And then you told them she ate the dog biscuits."

"Let me finish. I get a call from her sister that they're outside. We dim the lights. Everyone hides. The door opens, *Surprise!* and it's fantastic. She bear-hugs me, tells me she loves me, the first time she says this in front of people.

"Then I brought out the cake from her bedroom."

A porter walks through our car and confirms we've entered the Rockies. He's handsome, too handsome for this job. She smiles and watches as he passes.

"The cake's two tiers, a big circle and a smaller circle. Chocolate with chocolate frosting. I'd missed Chem lab to make it. Sparklers jutted out the top. Her name written in pink script. Big 'two' and 'zero' candles."

"And a Charco Snap," she said

"And a Charco Snap," I repeated. "Right next to her name. I'd gone to three stores to find them and still had to ask my mom to mail one. Our dog had died years before, but she'd kept them."

"That, hands down, is the oddest part of all this."

"Not really," I said. "Anyway, I emerge from the bedroom, carrying the cake, starting the song. Sparks fly, friends croon, and I can see it in this girl's eyes: *I. Love. You.* I was in. We were going to get married. We'd move in together senior year. We'd backpack all summer. She was going to be drunk and blow me when everyone left, if not right in the kitchen while everyone ate cake. I was in."

"Then . . . ."

"Then she sees the Charco Snap. Her expression plummets. I reach down and pull the thing out, but other people have seen it, ask why I'd placed a dog biscuit on the cake. They want to know. My roommates growl and bark."

"You told them, didn't you?"

"Of course! I was twenty! I decided if everyone knew the story, that she was just five, they'd let it go. An in-joke between us two. At the end of the song, she won't even blow out the big two and the big zero—so I try explaining."

"Slick."

"I know. Telling the story makes it worse, makes her bawl harder. She runs into her room. People who were laughing stopped laughing, then they leave. Her roommates go to console her. Her sister orders me to leave. My roommates take the cake, say it's better that way, eat it on their way out. I try pounding on her door, try apologizing. Her sister threatens to castrate me then call the cops. I step back, start cleaning up bottles and cans for some reason, then try again. Her sister calls the cops. I leave. That week, I call a million times, leave flowers and notes by her door, on her windshield, but that was it."

"Did you fly to Portland the day after Christmas?"

"On Christmas, I call her again, hoping for some holiday cheer. She answers. She wishes me Merry Christmas, asks how I did on my finals, then tells me, under no circumstance, am I to get on that plane. She's told her parents what happened and somehow, it came out that we'd also been fucking. Her dad will shoot me with his hunting rifle if I step foot in Oregon. I almost go anyway, but my mom won't drive me to the airport. I give up. I never talk to her again—she even dropped the classes we signed up for in the spring."

We didn't talk again for a while. The train zipped through caverns, along ledges, and at one point, through the middle of the tallest peak. We experienced absolute darkness. When things flattened out, somewhere near Vegas, she told me her story, how her first marriage ended. I knew she'd been married, but didn't know when, to whom, or how it'd ended. She detailed a fake pregnancy, a fake miscarriage, the guy paying off her credit cards and student loans in between. He was a weatherman for the local NBC affiliate and had weatherman money. I could picture him when she said his name. They were married two months. He'd been a mark the whole time.

"I was young," she said.

"Like twenty-five?"

"Thirty-three." A year before we'd met.

When we stopped in Vegas for a layover, she proposed this: Get off, stay in Vegas, pick the train back up on its way back. We could get a cheap room, screw like rabbits, eat at buffets.

"I thought you wanted to go to Tijuana?"

"More than Vegas?"

"Our things are stowed."

"They'll hold them. Will they even know we've gone?"

When I hesitated, she suggested a wedding. "We could invite strangers, hire a DJ."

"I can't dance," I said.

"Someone dressed like Elvis could do it. We could get flowers, a cake, a white dress and a tux. I'll walk down the aisle. We can lose money on slots and drink for free."

I knew right then that she wasn't getting back on the train, with or without me, not now or in six days. The porter made a last call, *All aboard.* We had two minutes. In two minutes, I could tell her the real worst thing I'd ever done, then let her decide whether or not we'd get back on. I knew my answer before I even got started.

# WHEN THE HEROES CAME TO TOWN

The consensus, among many of us, was that we were unimpressed. Before the heroes, things weren't that bad, and, depending on whom you asked, they were going pretty well. The county had just paid to have the throughway resurfaced, our boys had made it to the state semis, and business boomed at the tire factory up by the mall, which, in turn, made business boom at the mall as well. Everyone felt confident about the economy, the kids were getting into good colleges, and if a town with prettier women existed, we hadn't been there.

Which is why we scratched our heads when these heroes showed up, their jaws, their capes, their stoicism all in tow. We had to admit, their debut was a splash, putting the fire out at the tire factory. The dark cloud lifted after three days, the smell of soot and rot disappearing soon after. To boot, they maintained the integrity of the structure, limiting the shutdown to a mere week and a half. A few days later, they saved that kid who'd fallen into the quarry, too, not one of *our* boys, but a kid nonetheless. Not one of us could have squeezed into that drainage pipe, let alone pounded through the twenty solid feet of bedrock. Our hats were off. And tipped. Whether or not we could have fought off the supervillains and their giant mechanical attack birds isn't worth discussing. The talons alone were fourteen feet long, for chrissakes. We had to give them that one.

Cats out of trees and baby-kissing aside, we felt skeptical of the overall picture—skeptical at best. The heroes, for all their wondrous deeds, never really warmed up to us on a personal level. When their job was done, they disappeared, gone to whatever cave or fortress it was they called home, danger and wrongdoing at bay. No kind words, no interviews, not even a catchphrase to distinguish themselves. After the attack birds, someone came up with the idea of a picnic—horseshoes and sack races and potato salad—just to say thanks, to let them know we appreciated their efforts. That we noticed. That we had their backs. But the heroes, as smug as they were dashing, didn't even respond to the invitations. Not even a "No," and we'd sent stamped response postcards. "Peril never takes a break," a general statement later pronounced, "so neither can we." We started to think that they were saving our lives simply so they could mock us. *A picnic*, they laughed in their damp cave-lairs, between pushup contests. *Who do these people think they're dealing with?*

The women, of course, were quick to defend the heroes, reminding us of how hard it is to be the new kid on the block, how we'd feel the same way if we were the strangers and the heroes were the Welcome Wagon. Being our wives didn't obligate them to take our sides, but still. We were grateful for what the heroes had done—don't get us wrong—but when a man's wife starts to see the other guy's point of view, you begin to wonder just where her loyalties lie.

Our women's allegiance in question, suspicion arose. Who were these guys under the masks? Where did they come from? Why did they choose our town, out of all the towns in the world?

We didn't place an ad. We didn't throw up any signals. We weren't in any particular danger. We did, however, have the prettiest ladies. And any hero we'd ever seen always had a pretty lady hanging off at least one arm. Maybe the heroes weren't mocking us. Maybe they were auditioning. A few of the old-timers, those guys who hang out at the library, suggested that the heroes were responsible for the fire and the kid in the quarry, and anyone who bought into that theory had no trouble throwing in the giant, mechanical attack birds. Why not? It was all starting to make sense.

But as quickly as the heroes arrived, they left our town with even less of a flourish. No one knew they were gone, not until the tragedy at the dynamite plant. As the flames inched toward the main warehouse amidst explosions and screaming and mayhem, everyone watched the skies, assuming the heroes would swoop in to save the day. We'd all be safe, the women would swoon, and the heroes would leave without saying a word. Several large, disastrous explosions later, it finally hit us: No one was going to dig a fjord to the lake in the hills to drown out the fires, and no mighty wind was going to blow out the hundreds of thousands of fuses, sizzling and snapping and sparkling. The heroes weren't coming. No one was. We were on our own.

The women took the news of the heroes' departure the hardest (except for the families of the dynamite victims, of course). Our wives wept openly. To be honest, it was the reaction we had expected.

More surprising, however, was how close they held us at night, with a firmer grip, almost desperate, closer and tighter than any one of us remembered being held before. While it's nice to be wanted, it felt more like a mixed blessing. Some of us had left town for this and that before. Did our wives hold our empty pillows like they held us when the heroes left? Did they stare at our pictures? We weren't sure if we wanted to know the answers to these questions, but there they were. One day, we might have posed these questions to our wives, but until we were ready to make that move, we held fast. The economy was still OK and our kids were still getting into good schools. The heroes were gone and they didn't seem to be coming back. Though we could never be sure whom it was our wives held so closely, we were there for them, and always would be. It was in these moments, our wives in our arms, their minds off in the skies, that we were the heroes, living hero lives, enjoying vicarious rewards. We were just returning the favor, there for our women, posing as our own secret identities.

# PREGNANT WITH PEANUT BUTTER

This was how Agnes described the sandwich when I asked her how much peanut butter she'd put on. That was her answer, like the bread was with child. Like it glowed.

"To make it count," she said.

One sliver of one peanut would kill me. When you're as allergic as I am, the amount wouldn't matter—you either die or you don't.

Agnes was my pharmacist. Every three months, my epinephrine injectors expired and I needed to reload. I'd buy dozens, keeping two on my person and one in my house at all times.

"Have you ever gone into shock?" she said.

"Once, as a baby," I said. "I don't remember it."

"Fascinating," she said, sliding my debit card through the slot. "Come over tonight."

No woman had ever propositioned me. I hadn't been on a date in years.

"Eight o'clock," she said, looking behind me to the next guy in line.

"Where do you live?" I asked.

"See you at eight."

Agnes was beyond what I considered my range. She looked like an actress playing a pharmacist in a movie. Her white coat seemed like something the store made her wear to cover her short skirts and plunging tops.

"Eight," she repeated as I walked away.

At eight, Agnes pulled into the parking lot of my complex. Then I recognized her car, her. She lived in the condo next door and entertained a lot, mostly men. I hadn't made the connection, not in three years, not without the white coat.

I spied out the peephole. As Agnes walked by, she mouthed "Eight," and made for her door. I had to shower. I had a date with Agnes, my neighbor-pharmacist.

The sandwich sat made on the kitchen counter when Agnes let me in. I stopped in the doorway as if it were a growling dog. I could be in the same room with it, as long as I didn't touch it. I'd read about a guy in Michigan who walked into a grocery store, a store that sold peanuts in bins along the back wall, a hundred yards away. The dust in the air was enough to do it. He died on the checkout conveyor. I'm not that sensitive.

"I've delayed this," Agnes said. "Since you live next door."

"Delayed what?" I asked.

Agnes finished a glass of wine. "Did you bring your shots?"

I carried my shots like I carried my wallets and keys. I said, "I can come back when you're done eating."

"Follow me," she said.

By the time I reached the bedroom, Agnes had undressed. The sandwich from the kitchen counter loomed on the credenza next to the bed.

That's when Agnes told me what we were going to do.

The timing would be crucial, Agnes explained. First, she'd fuck me. Nothing weird, nothing violent, though I could make requests. At the cusp of my climax, she'd feed me the sandwich. As my throat closed, as my skin hived, I'd come, the most magnificent, powerful, immaculate ejaculate of my life. Then she'd poke me with the shot and I'd be fine.

"I've always wondered if this would work," she said.

That's when I asked how much peanut butter she'd put on, when she used the word pregnant. She had nothing to lose and I could very well die.

"You should be on top," I said.

When I was nine, I was abducted. On the way to school, there was this house with a million trees and bushes out front. One morning, a man pulled me into the cover. I thought it was this kid from down the street, a bigger kid who was our paperboy and liked to torment me. But it was a strange guy wearing a wrestling mask. He put duct tape around my mouth and hands and carried me to the driveway where his red van was parked. We drove all day, stopping once for gas and once for McDonald's. When he reached his destination, it was dark and the tape on my mouth had come off.

"Why didn't you scream?" the guy asked when he noticed.

I shrugged. I was an agreeable kid.

He led me to a shed behind a house in the woods. Later, I became much more scared of that shed than I was when it was happening. When I was nine, I didn't know what kidnappers did to kids in sheds in the woods.

It never got that far. Inside the shed, the guy's brother and dad were working on something, a table maybe, doing things that should be done in sheds, sanding and pounding.

"Marvin, what the hell?" the brother said.

"You just got out," the dad said.

The dad went to the house to call the police and the brother smacked Marvin across the head. Marvin undid the tape and cried, apologizing. By the next day I was home and my parents never let me go anywhere alone again until I was seventeen. My mom insists this is why I haven't married. I'm thirty-nine. I think I'm over it.

"I thought it would work," Agnes said. "Like with a noose."

Three empty epinephrine vials lay next to me on the bed, along with my apartment key. I wiped sweat off my body with a pillow, catching my breath.

"It got stuck to the roof of my mouth," I said. "I thought that was a myth."

Agnes took the sandwich and disappeared. I dressed and followed.

"Up for a movie?" I said. "Dinner?"

Agnes was still nude, smoking, staring out her window. The news was on the TV.

"I liked the first part of it. Before the sandwich."

"You'll be back in tomorrow, for replacements," she said.

"First thing."

"Go in first thing," she said. "I work at four."

# MAN OF THE YEAR

1

The ballgame on the radio is in the 29$^{th}$ inning, a record. I started listening while driving to a banquet ceremony where I will receive a prestigious award, and I've been circling the hall for an hour. A backup shortstop is pitching for one team, tomorrow's scheduled starter for the other. The managers have sent the scratched players to the airport, both teams playing tomorrow out of town. The shortstop, a rookie from Cuba, is throwing 96 m.p.h. and has struck out four of five guys he's faced. The other pitcher is on his tenth inning of no-hit ball, the game of his life, but it won't count, not in that way. I should park and go inside, get my award, do the right thing, but I don't want to miss the end, hear it live. The smokers standing outside have seen me drive by, more than once, too. My cell has eighteen voicemails. My text inbox is full. Sixty people wait on me, but I'm not stopping.

2

When I was eleven, I lost my testicles in a game of freeze tag. For some reason, we had a safety base, superfluous in freeze tag, because if you get tagged, you just wait for someone to unfreeze you. The base was overdoing it. But we had one, the fire hydrant in front of my house, painted red, white, and blue for the bicentennial the summer before. I'd just been freed—I think it was my sister who saved me, or maybe she was it—so I bolted toward the hydrant as soon as I could move, not caring about the other frozen kids, not bothering to save them. Whoever was it tagged me as I reached the hydrant and pushed me forward, my balls in line with one of the protruding valves. There was a sound: It included my jeans ripping, me gasping for breath, the clank of my knees against the metal. I exhaled and started screaming, other kids started screaming, and my sister ran into the house. My dad came out, he saw me on the sidewalk, then he started screaming. The doctors didn't have much to work with, but made me look presentable, for which I'm grateful. The next summer, we moved, and the first time we drove to the new house, I asked, "There's isn't a fire hydrant out front, is there?" "No," my mom said, then I heard her whisper to my dad, "Not that it matters now."

### 3

"People breathe oxygen, exhale carbon dioxide. Plants take in the $CO_2$, absorb the carbon, then release oxygen for us to breathe. It's how air works. I also know that if we're trapped in an airtight space, we will suffocate. But, I wonder what would happen if we were trapped in said space with plants: How much longer would we last? How many plants would it take to keep up with us, to recycle enough air for us to breathe? Thank you for this fabulous honor. Good night and drive safely." This is the acceptance speech I have planned for when I go inside, for the podium. It'll get everyone thinking, make them applaud, give them something to talk about on the way home. Two hours after cocktails, dessert served and tables cleared, I won't be giving a speech. The game is in the $32^{nd}$ inning. The pitcher with ten no-hit innings hit a home run in the top of the 31$^{st}$, but gave one up in the bottom half with two outs, an 0-2 pitch. These were the first runs since the 4$^{th}$. Twenty-six scoreless innings broken up, but onward they play.

4

Girls in high school, some in college, assumed I was gay. They wondered why I wouldn't date, why I didn't try, why I didn't ogle them or make high school-boy comments. Trina Lipowski, at music camp the summer before college, got my secret out of me. We were first and second chair coronet, and one night, imbibed with peppermint schnapps, I told her. She took me up as a challenge, spending most nights imploring for her chance. I insisted it was impossible, but she wouldn't budge: She wanted her shot, said she wouldn't give up, even if it took all summer.

5

The Commissioner calls into the radio broadcast. He is on vacation, someplace where it's daytime, speaking from beside a pool. There is no protocol for this, he explains. It's up to the home plate umpire's discretion to call the game or play on. The radio announcer posits that since he's Commissioner, there should be something he can do, but the Commissioner insists this is good for the game. He calls himself a fan, like all of us, says he's enjoying the epic battle. As he signs off, I find that I agree with him. The game is in the 38$^{th}$ inning. For the visitors, all three outfielders are starting pitchers, the three not scheduled for today or tomorrow. For the home team, the catcher has moved to third and the third baseman, a catcher in high school, is catching. A ball heads for the bleachers, seemingly the game-winner, but it hooks foul at the last moment. The next pitch, the batter strikes out. I would have bet

24

my life that this was going to happen after the long foul, but no one else is in the car with whom to bet.

## 6

The night before camp ended, down on the dock, Trina convinced me to show her. She pulled down my shorts, examined me with her blue eyes, flicked it with her finger. Nothing. She removed her bikini top, and in the moonlight, I touched the first and last live breasts I have seen to date. She approved, her feet dangling in the lake, my fingers moving like I was playing my horn. I could see the attraction, what guys saw in this, but I didn't have the parts. I stopped when I got bored. Trina cried as she retied her strings. I said, "Don't feel bad. They're great." "I'm crying for you," she said. "They are great. Every girl's are."

## 7

After the 41$^{st}$ inning, the umpires and managers converge at the plate. The announcer is predicting suspension, but then shouts, "They're calling the players onto the field!" The game is over nine hours old. All of my friends have left the banquet hall, some of them driving behind, in front of, or next to me as I make a pass. I wave until I note nobody waves back. I circle the block four times after the last car leaves, park under the rain canopy. My trophy sits outside with a note attached: "We took a poll—your brakes and your cell phone are both broken." There is an inscription on the base, which I'll read later, but I assume it's nice. They wouldn't have had time to change it.

## 8

It's possible, Trina Lipowski, points out, that I am gay. I hadn't heard from her in twenty-four years, not since a letter the first week of college, ten days after the dock. She found me online. We exchanged catch-ups. Within a day, she wrote, "Maybe you're gay. That thing happened when you were nine—you never had the chance to find out. That's why I contacted you: because I thought of that." The next e-mail in my box, from management, told me about the award. I wrote back to Trina, asking her to the dinner, to be my date. She never wrote back.

9

I drive toward home, my trophy in my trunk, and run out of gas halfway there. I'd had a full tank when I started. In the moonlight on the edge of the road, I listen to the game, entering the $47^{th}$ inning, midnight come and gone. All gas stations in town are closed. I wonder how long I have, listening to the radio, until the battery dies. I want to call someone for help, for a ride, to take me to a TV or another radio. This time, no one waits me out.

# SHELF LIFE

I sit, stuck to the couch, the TV tuned to the Monday night game, half a sixer on the floor next to my feet, the empties spread about. The burglars break in, I belch in greeting, they nod.

They hit the typicals first: the silverware, my wife's jewelry box, the mini-grandfather with the busted chime. Next go the gadgets—the blender, popcorn popper, food processor, and bread maker—four anniversary gifts, never used, on display in a row under the sink.

When I open a beer, the production line out to the van halts, burglars rubbernecking. I offer my last two, common courtesy where I was raised. They thank me and take a break to catch a few plays.

Halftime. The microwave remains, a jar of nacho cheese spinning and bubbling for our dipping needs. The electronics go next: My new friends appropriate the PlayStation, stereo components, DVD player, and digital camera. After another break—cheese-covered nachos and the third quarter—they make reference to the TV.

"Sure is a beaut. Musta cost you a fortune."

A 52-inch console, I tell them. Tube's on its last leg, but still the best on the block, save those flat screens. They can't lift it on their own, they soon discover, but with my volunteered assistance, it's no problem. Again, common courtesy.

My pride and joy follows me into their van, me pulling, the perps pushing, all the way to the front of the cargo hold, trapping me inside. The van doors slam shut, leaving me in the dark, no outlet for the TV, no couch to sit on, no salty snacks waiting on the coffee table. I yell and pound, but there's no response. Nothing. After an hour on the road, the wheels begin to turn: Does anyone even know I'm back here? What a laugh we'll have when they open the doors and find me inside!

The doors finally part. Light shines in and I sense the city: sewers, spicy sandwiches, streetlights, the screeching of the subway. Without any big laughs, my console and I are introduced to Larry, who smells of menthol and rum, in the following fashion: a 36-inch color console, good condition; a thirty-six-year-old male, married, between jobs, possibly alcohol dependent. Larry talks them down, and after a bit of haggling, I say good-bye to the boys.

The next step: disguise. Larry shaves me hairless then covers me with two coats of whitewash. My fingertips—the prints—are sanded off, which Larry apologizes for more than once. I remind him of DNA testing and Larry describes me as petty larceny, very unworthy of DNA-equipped law enforcement officers.

"This is not TV," he explains. "No Robert Stack with your mug on the tube."

My mug, however, is the real problem, he points out. He winds his fist and breaks my nose, again profusely apologizing. He says the shave needed supplementing. Two weeks locked in the back room will help, until things cool.

My ultimate destination: the shelf with the lamps, neon beer lights, and a widow from Lexington. I do not sell, or, in Larry's language, move. Some creep walks in, maybe once every week or two, examines the price tag on my ass, then leaves. I wait on the shelf for months. I begin to doubt my self-worth; Larry refuses to come down, whatever the tag says. I find his faith in me reassuring.

Then one day my wife walks in. She is accompanied by someone other than me, another gentleman. She doesn't notice me, concentrating on the glass counter by the register. She points and pencils figures into a pad while the other man wraps his arms around her waist. She smiles and pokes at his ribs. I cannot hear what they say, but when my wife removes her wedding band and slides it across the glass to Larry, I know the score.

"Marjorie," I yell out. "Don't do this, baby."

"Quiet," Larry calls in my general direction. "I don't want the merchandise hassling my customers."

Marjorie saunters towards me. The other man begins to follow, but she signals for him to stay.

"Do I know you?"

I explain my abduction, the burglars, Larry's disguise. She looks at me like she did the items in the glass case, squinting her soft blue eyes, pricing.

"I assumed you stole all our stuff and left me," she says.

"Of course I didn't leave you, baby." A tear drips down my cheek and falls to the floor. It's cloudy white with whitewash. I hold out my arms.

Marjorie embraces me as white stains her amber hair. The moment ends when Marjorie tips me on my side and peeks at my tag. After a second, she levels me back on the shelf and nods. With a peck on my forehead, she returns to her escort. When she pulls money out of her wallet and passes it to Larry, I am positive I'm being purchased, that I'm headed home. Larry puts the money in his sock next to his 9 mm Beretta, then marches over and unmounts me from my shelf. I say farewell to the lady from Lexington, who does not respond, despondent, the last pup in the litter.

Instead of moving me out to the strange man's car, Larry places me on a new shelf, near the back of the store, amid an array of TVs, including my 52-inch color console, its fading tube replaced, its woodlike casing polished to a shine. I ask Larry what's up. He reminds me to keep quiet.

From my new shelf, I watch Marjorie resume the pawning of her ring. Larry takes the money out of his sock, plus more from the drawer. Then Marjorie's lover leads her out. I scream her name despite Larry's threat. Marjorie does not look back.

After some deliberation, I decide Marjorie did not have the money to cover my tag, that she is somewhere, scrimping, saving, our wedding ring a deposit on my rescue. I wait, longing for another embrace, for one more look into her beautiful blue eyes, the sweet smell of her soft hair, the seductive sound of her voice, the comfort of knowing that I am part of something, of two people who were made for each other, to live in love until the end of time. Man and wife. I ask Larry to plug in my 52-incher and go get us some beer.

# THE LAST TIME WE HAD INTERCOURSE

The last time we had intercourse, my wife used the wrong uterus and that's how she got herself pregnant. We weren't trying to conceive, and in fact, to ensure we'd stay childless, we took every precaution: I stayed on top, no kissing, no prayer before or after, and I made sure I lasted less than a minute. Personally, I'd done everything right. That's why I'm furious with Grace. And I know: If only I'd taken this negative energy into the bedroom, we wouldn't be in this mess. No matter how badly my wife screwed up.

The pastor at our church insisted we keep the baby. In fact, he volunteered to counsel us to ensure nothing ungodly came to pass. Before Grace and I had even talked about it, Reverend Pasquale and his wife Joannie were sitting in our living room, eating Grace's duck liver pâté, playing Taboo, and instructing us on how to childproof our apartment. The plugs would need caps, the table corners were too pointy, and my stacks of CDs would have to go. Grace was excited to have guests, our first in eight years, especially the good preacher and his wife. What was weird, not keeping the baby hadn't crossed my mind, not until Reverend Pasquale stopped us on the way out of service last week. He was flummoxed by the notion of planting such vileness in my head, his face turning the color of the pâté. Joannie said, "You could put a changing table right where that TV is. You need to be able to change in every room."

When I was a kid, my dad gave me the Talk while we waited in line for a roller coaster. He explained the plumbing first, noting the different chambers, going into detail about pipes, wrenches, and reservoirs. Once I was able to repeat every part of both my own self and my future wife's, he switched tracks and demonstrated attitudes, techniques, even pillow talk, the difference between a child-rearing disposition and the other kind. By the time we reached the front of the line—I now a man, the smaller kids in line damaged for life—I knew three things: 1) If I ever had kids, both parties would have to consent; 2) No matter what happened, I was in charge; and 3) Why would I ever want to have marital relations when there were awesome things like baseball, bicycles, and roller coasters in the world?

After doing some research and consulting with my father, I was certain my Grace had planned this pregnancy. I thought back to that fatal afternoon, running through scenarios over and over again. There was no way the combination I used should have failed, angry, fast, and missionary as effective as outright sterility. It had to be her, her cunning. At the outset of her last trimester, I accused Grace of conspiring against me and she denied it, swearing the conception was the Lord's work. She then asked me if I loved our unborn baby, if I was grateful to the Lord for this gift. I told her I was grateful, and all of sudden, she turned the tables. She asked if *I* was the one who'd planned this, if *I* had propagated without permission. Dear Lord, the doubt crept up inside me right then. Maybe I'd angled myself incorrectly. Maybe I'd thought about babies during climax. Worst of all, there could have been love in my heart.

Within seconds, Grace was locked in her bedroom, sobbing and calling her sister, and I was questioning my own self: *Did* I plan that baby? *Had* I done everything in my power? I became so confused, I could no longer remember what'd transpired that day. Who initiated the coitus? Was I wearing my maroon pajamas? And most important of all: Which testicle had the sperm come from, the left or the right?

*—for Todd A.*

# LAX

I flew back to Dallas when the dog died prematurely from plastic surgery. Tucking Boxer's jowls was my ex's brilliance, giving him a permanent grin. I thought Boxer was happy all along. But Veronica, seven procedures rich, claimed Boxer felt more dated than venerable, and declared that he, too, deserved eternal youth. Boxer bit through his neck the morning after, the meds goofing his depth perception, those stitches itching like shit. I wanted to say, "At least he died with a smile on his face," but saved it. Boxer was my boy. I reserved the quips for my ex.

I knew I wasn't immortal when I starting pissing after showers. I'd been trained to go before—Veronica almost killed me when she caught me pissing down the drain—but one day I stepped from the stall and needed to piss again. This preceded the nose hairs, ear hairs, the paunch, even the gray. I went to Veronica to tell her, but she picked that moment to drop her bomb and said she was leaving me for the young fellow who taught her tennis. The next morning, I pissed twice, once in the shower, again in Veronica's gym bag.

At Boxer's vigil, the plastic surgeon appeared baffled by Boxer's demise, the physics of biting one's own neck. "Maybe it wasn't Boxer who bit Boxer," I said, so many other dogs in

34

the neighborhood, maybe a fox or opossum smelling the salt in the sutures.

The vet took it as a jab. "Veronica's a saint," he said. "She's lucky she's moved on." During the eulogy, my daughter held a candle, looked broken, while my son whispered it was good I came because Boxer loved me best. I'd said this during the divorce, wanting Boxer when Veronica'd gotten the kids. "Who steals a dog from his children?" she said. I wanted to reply, "Who takes kids from their father?" but instead asked, "How's that backhand?"

On the plane back, I met a man who'd just tried to buy the Dallas Cowboys and steal them to LA. He said his price was fair, but Jerry wasn't budging. "Stubborn bastard," he said. I wondered why he had that kind of scratch but flew commercial. I told the man about my dog, the procedure, how Boxer was only eleven and still had good years left. "Bullshit," the man said. "There's no such thing." I wanted to get up and piss, but the seat belt light told me no. When I couldn't take it anymore, I pulled a hanky from my pocket, tied it around my face like a bandit, tapped the billionaire on the shoulder. I said, "If you think you're leaving this plane with that billion dollars, you got another think coming," pointing my fingers at him like six-shooters. The man raised his hands in surrender and I picked up the briefcase at his feet. It'd be a tough getaway, but I could start anew when we landed, if I could just make it across the border. Behind my mask, the law on my trail, I'd smile the entire way.

# MILO HIMES

Milo Himes disappeared from a Utah beach one Wednesday last month. It's possible he wandered too far out and drowned in the undertow, but the police suspect foul play, someone grabbing him then disappearing over the dunes. Drifters and local sex offenders top their list. The media thinks it's the stepmom, playing up how she stayed at the beach four hours after reporting him gone. Me? I'm wondering why no one's saying "shark." That lake in Utah, it's salt, so why not? I call the police. The police hang up. There's no cash reward involved—I just want to help. If there's a great white in the Great Salt, it could strike again at any time.

On the home front, it starts with tiny red ants. I find a gap between the faucet unit and the countertop where the seal has disintegrated. Or been melted. Or chewed. I paper-towel the ants, make it all white again, but every time I get a drink of water, go to the fridge, or take a pill, I see a thousand more. I wipe them up, they come back. I clean, they come back. I put out traps, they have a little party. I spray my entire house with vinegar, sixteen bottles of Heinz, and after a few days, they're gone. I recaulk the sink, do the same in the bathroom tub, too. I have defeated the tiny red ants.

The Great Salt Lake contains no sharks: I checked the Internet. But other lakes in the world do. Bull sharks in Africa can live in fresh water. They take a wrong turn at a channel and can't find their way home. For some reason, they produce twenty times more urine than bull sharks living in saltwater. I'm pretty sure it's the opposite for people: salt = peeing. I think of my father's prostate, his need to go every ten minutes. I picture him in a saltwater tank in his living room, wearing a scuba mask and oxygen tanks. He's floating in his red-and-blue trunks, giving a thumbs-up, watching a game, reaching over the side of the tank for a shot of rye, to dip a chip in dip. He doesn't have the money for that kind of contraption, and I'm guessing his insurance wouldn't pay for it, either. And Milo Himes didn't disappear in Africa.

Next is a mouse in the cupboard. At least I hope it's a mouse and not a rat—I've never seen either. Bags of rice, of flour, of tea are gnawed through. Black shit dashes my linoleum. Floury steps lead to a hole in the baseboard behind the stove. I duct-tape it shut; two days later, the tape has been bored through. I set traps; they're picked clean. I get a cat; it runs away. I buy D-Con, shove it in the hole, nail a new board over the opening. I sit in the dark and listen, hear something scuffling, struggling. They are inside the cardboard packaging, eating the poison. That's the last I hear from any of them. The reek from their carcasses lasts a couple days, but smells, no matter how nasty, can't eat my food.

Milo Himes' left shoe is found in a diner bathroom in Green River, southern part of the state. They know it's his because descriptions have been all over the news, his shoes distinctive, Elmo and Big Bird, arm in wing, Milo's doodles on the toes. A janitor spotted it behind a toilet. I think the janitor's got Milo, to be honest, because it's always the janitor, some ex-con or mental patient. He just happened to spot this shoe and turn it in? Fuck me. But I used to be a janitor, at a school, and I never did it.

When she hired me, the superintendent told me never to smile at the kids, never talk to them. I obeyed. Last fall, some girl showed signs of abuse, said it was her dad, and the first thing he said when they questioned him? "It's probably some janitor at school." The police questioned me in the kindergarten for two hours, treating me like I was feeling her up right there on the tiny desks. They brought up my B&E from when I was seventeen—I pinched a couple of car stereos—and somehow tied that to raping third-graders twenty years later. But they had nothing on me, and eventually, the dad got caught, in his daughter's bed, both of them sobbing and naked. A week later, I was laid off. The superintendent said she was getting too many calls. Parents didn't want me around, even though an aunt had walked in on the scene and the dad hung himself in lockup that night.

I'm pretty sure I have squirrels in my attic. They move around during the day, then hit the town in full dark. I sit in my yard at dusk one night and watch: They're raccoons. There's a hole right under the gutter, southeast corner. Two coons use it like a revolving door, living in sin in my attic. I make some calls—raccoons will claw your fingernails out, then give you rabies. One exterminator says he can handle it, but it will cost me $380. I clean my rifle. I give the raccoons one more night together—I imagine them at a midnight chapel, tying the knot, having a final roll in a Dumpster—then pick them off at dawn when they cross my property line: two shots, two kills. I'm burying them in the garden when three squad cars pull up and six cops jump out, vests on, guns drawn, screaming for me to get on the ground, to drop my *motherfucking* shovel or else I'm *fucking* dead. They see my Winchester on the porch and take it and me in. They inform me I can't shoot at mammals, or anything, even on my own property, within city limits. The judge doles out my fine—$2,400—plus I have to surrender the Winchester. I wonder if this judge isn't the bastard who married those raccoons. Vengeance comes full circle, I guess, and I surrender my life savings to the clerk, just so I can go home and see what else has made its move.

Milo Himes is never found. The stepmom and the dad divorce, which seems like a clue, but tragedy results in so many divorces, the experts say, so maybe not. A few months later, it comes out that the stepmom went to high school with that janitor's first cousin. A lot is made of that. But Utah is small, people-wise, and everyone knows everybody. I want to believe that Milo is somewhere, in a well-lit room, eating Trix, drinking a juice box, watching cartoons, asking when he can go home, but less frequently than he did before. I want his captors to love him, to simply have wanted a little Milo for their own. Maybe Milo loves them back by now. Maybe he never liked his stepmom to begin with. Maybe his dad drank. Whatever the case, I hope they find these people who took him. So much trauma, to the dad, to the family, to the police. And to me. If something bad happened to Milo, the likely case, I hope it's a swift trial, that the defendants don't appeal, just take their medicine, do the honorable thing. They still have firing squads in Utah, I read, and that gives me hope.

I wake up to some noises coming from downstairs. It's three weeks after the raccoons, and I only have my mom's old handgun—sadly, no bullets. I walk downstairs and find a guy stuck in one of the side windows, his huge ass unable to wiggle free. He's trying to reach the floor, grab onto the radiator pipes off to the side. I kick him in the cheek. He reaches back like he's got something to use on me, but I cock my empty Glock under his nose and he goes limp, half of him in my dining area, half of him outside. I find a .22 in his waistband put it in my belt. I ask what he's doing, and he says he saw my TV from the street, my plasma.

"You were going to carry it out the window?"

"I was going to unlock the door."

I'm pretty certain I can shoot an intruder—an armed one especially—once they cross the threshold. I tell him this and he begs me not to kill him, suggests I call the police. I consider it, but instead go and get my duct tape, my boards and nails, and the tub of Plaster of Paris. I tie the guy's hands and start sealing him in, taping him up, boarding the window. He tells me the blood is going to his head, that he's going to faint. I give him a glass of water from the sink, a banana, and a granola bar— the corner chewed off—from the cupboard. I tell him his new name is Fido. He says that someone will see his legs, half a man hanging out my window. He says he has to go to the bathroom. He asks why my house smells like vinegar. I tell him that nobody lives next door, and soon, I'll go out and cover his legs with a tarp, make him look like a stack of firewood. I tell him to go to the bathroom, just let it fly. He eats the banana and asks if this is his last meal. I tell him no, he caught me at a good point in my life.

"There's been enough killing," I say.

As soon as the cast dries, I go upstairs and sleep, more soundly than I have since I can remember.

# INSTEAD OF GETTING MARRIED

Instead of getting married, I insisted that Julian and I rig an election. This came as great distress to my parents, Dad especially, me pregnant, the hall already booked. But if we didn't do it now, we'd have to wait another four years, and by then, who knew where our interests would lie? Hokey vows and the hokey pokey could wait, and Dad, given either a grandson or an upper-class tax cut, would forgive all.

Our date decided, we put a deposit down on a local hopeful, boyish and Protestant, instructing him to stand by his party on every issue, tan no more than once a week, and above all else, have intercourse exclusively with his wife. His opponent, the incumbent, proved less cooperative, given the exact set of instructions, only opposite. But as our parents told us, being an honest politician wasn't easy—it was something you had to work at your whole life. We didn't have our whole lives, but together, I knew Julian and I could accomplish anything.

Come spring, our man didn't *exist* in the polls, placing third behind a Libertarian running from jail. Misfortune soon befell the beloved six-termer, however, and ours began to rise. His chin was a '75 Buick, looking like his opponent's quarterback grandson, and during debates, he spoke simply, spouting colloquialisms the media deemed "mistakes." But he was real, a man you either fished with or voted for in November. Pulling a pregnant woman from the path of a speeding car didn't hurt his image, either. By July, our man had jumped the incarcerated third-partier, pulling within six percent overall. I asked Julian if he still wanted to go through with it, and he told me he was never more sure of anything in his life. That night, we felt the baby kick for the first time, and somehow, I knew we couldn't lose.

By late October, the state started seeing the six-termer as a relic, and thanks to the money we borrowed from the mob, our man's face graced more TV ads and lawn signs than there were registered voters. Around Halloween, Julian started to get cold feet, us in cahoots with such deviants, but I assured him it was all on the up-and-up. This was a lie, but lies are what good relationships, like campaigns, are built on.

During our man's acceptance speech the following Tuesday, my water broke. Julian, holding my hand in the back of the ambulance, proposed again. Before I could answer, a contraction came, giving me time to think. Fifty percent of marriages, like two-party campaigns, end poorly, and since we were already one for one, Julian and I appeared doomed. But if recent experience had taught me anything, it was that odds can be bent in your favor. The contraction subsided and I pulled Julian to my ear, whispering instructions, all but ensuring victory come June.

# HIGH TREASON

Against my better judgment, I attend this week's meeting of the Fuzzy Stuffed Animal Candy Council. The meeting starts five minutes late—they were waiting for someone—then they take roll. Though I've been there once or twice before, no one on the Council gives me a look, all eyes forward, all business. I start to think I don't belong, but remember the meetings are open to the public, and I'm entitled to witness the proceedings.

Popo the Panda introduces the first order of business: the seating arrangement on the toy chest. Popo states that the bears are tired of the back row, against the wall, and how some of the other Council members, because space is tight, are forced to lie across their laps. Popo's motion calls for open seating, plus permission to move the excess members to the white dresser by the window. Cinnamon, Honey, and Smokie all second Popo's motion. In the end, four votes aren't enough. For another week, the bears will anchor the back row of the toy chest.

The next item, presented by Gil Gorilla, addresses the growing discord between the stuffed animals and the dolls. Gil's first beef is how the dolls get to sit at their meeting table ad infinitum, complete with full tea set, while the stuffed animals get nothing. Worse, with the exception of a random bow tie, top hat, or felt vest, the stuffed animals live in the nude, while the dolls not only get to wear clothes—lacy dresses and bountiful bonnets—but all of them have *changes* of clothes, folded in the bottom drawer of the white dresser by the window. Snapper Gator, Council Chair, attempts to keep heads cool, suggesting a fairness committee be formed to evaluate the best course of action. So many of the dolls are children, she reminds us, and no one's suggesting any aggressive action towards a child at this juncture. Butterfly Betsy flaps her wings to second, and the Council, sated by the proposal of the fairness committee, moves forward.

After a short recess, the Council brings forth an array of smaller, less-pressing issues. They discuss painting the playroom to look like a forest or jungle, perhaps a combination of both. A Council member, who asks to remain anonymous, proposes lifting the ban on intermaterial marriages, while Button Eyes the Bunny suggests a smoking ban, good for within a hundred yards of the playroom—for the first time, I feel the Council's eyes drawn to me. Gil Gorilla calls for more money in the nightlight fund, and when Jennifer the Pink Polka-Dotted Giraffe inquires as to where in "the hell" this extra nightlight money would come from, Gil suggests they bump the sin tax on honey to eight percent, which only makes the teddy bears more furious, the last thing anyone wanted. The meeting adjourns and the animals move back to the toy chest to pursue their personal agendas.

Dinner isn't ready when my wife comes home, her first day back at work. I feel awful. This meal was the only imperative for the day, and for some reason, I'd promised her something extra special. It won't be. I microwave-defrost freezer-burned chicken, sprinkle it with oregano, old white zinfandel serving as marinade. As it bakes, she tells me they got a new printer, and that no one talked to her unless they had to, the ladies' room, the break room, et cetera, but still, it wasn't as bad as she'd imagined.

My wife then asks me what I did all day. I tell her that I did the dinner dishes from the night before, which I did, threw a load of darks in, including her black dress, which I did, and talked to my parents on the phone for quite a while, which isn't quite as true as the first two. I consider telling her about the Council Meeting, all the issues on the table, but we'd talked about these meetings a few days before, how she didn't think it was a good idea that I go anymore, that maybe it was best I steer clear of the playroom altogether. I don't tell my wife about the Council meeting, because of this talk, but also because my wife does not tell me, in that great of detail, what she did all day, nor did I expect a real answer when I asked her how her day was.

Most of all, I don't tell my wife about the Fuzzy Stuffed Animal Candy Council meeting because, if I'm not mistaken, her loyalties lie with the dolls. The stuffed animals spoke openly in my presence, confided in me their intentions, and while I didn't sign a gag order or even pinky swear, giving secrets to the enemy is the worst kind of treason. While my wife sides with the dolls, their pretty dresses in large part supplied by her, I side with the stuffed animals, see their point of view. After all, they have some pretty legitimate concerns.

# THE OLD COUNTRY

The whole-kernel corn lives on the station with the meats and gravies. The other vegetables wait undisturbed on the salad bar, which I visit only to fetch the ranch dressing I need for chicken drummettes. But to corn, I succumb: yellow, precious, life-giving, heart-mending. One heaping ladle always finds my plate, and with ample salt and butter, I can consume it, even sop its juices with its brethren, corned bread.

Another purity lives among the meats, this one more precious than any golden harvest: my Bernadette. As I pile chicken—fried, broasted, barbecued, and teriyaki—my Bernadette smiles, carving knife in hand, foot-tall chef's hat floating on maize hair like a foot-tall halo. By the time I reach the loins, I can see the mole hiding on her left eyelid, her kernel of beauty, my immaculate *pani* waiting to render roasted beef for the third of my plate I reserve especially for her offerings.

I've come to this establishment for the past thirty-nine days now—sometimes at both lunch and dinner, for the unlimited portions and home-cooking atmosphere, yes, but mostly to see my Bernadette. I fill my life with many pleasures, most from this restaurant, and she is the pleasure I most crave, the angel at the end of the line, the person I long to see across from me in the booth made not for one, but two. I've not yet spoken with her, nothing aside from traditional greetings: "Medium rare today, yes?" or demands for her craft: "No, two. And ham." But my Bernadette, she knows my face, one, like hers, from the old country, rounded, with a crooked nose and thin lips, a Pole in search of America—of freedom, of desire, of dreams come true, of everything you can eat in one sitting. Now, on my fortieth day, I am ready to free myself from suffering, to ask my Bernadette if she'll sit with me on her next night off and break of my dinner roll, sip of my bottomless soda.

When my destiny's glance falls upon me, her knife glides another three quarters of an inch across the festal beast—lamb tonight—and begins to carve a thick slab, her forearm toned, like veal, a product of her artistry. Ergo, she knows not why I am here—not for her meat, no, but for her.

"My name is Janusz Crapowski," I say, breaking my silence. "But *pani*, you may call me 'Hugo.'"

My Bernadette's slicing slows, and for an instance, her mole disappears, revealing eyes—blue pools eclipsed by black suns— eyes that meet my own.

"*Nie mowiem po ingolsz*," she says.

My heart hums as I drift into grammatical lessons in green grasses, vocabulary drills amidst Vermont ski lodges, conjugations of all verbs on sandy beaches. I undo the buttons on my red shirt, Hawaiian, tight and unbearable against my girth, my mind lost in dreams of her soft touch.

My visions end only with a skipped beat, of visions come true: My Bernadette's hand reaches out to touch me! Her finger extends, as if waiting for a ring, and suddenly: Contact! A fingertip of her rubber-glove penetrates my open shirt, reaching the center of my being, of my soul, the bounty of Bernadette's offerings: my hair-covered stomach. For an instant, I feel my true purpose has reared itself and my pani and I are to become as one.

At the same time as this contact, however, Bernadette points with her other hand, not to any of my other bountiful parts, but to a sign next to the cashier's register, a sign reading "NO SHIRT NO SHOES NO SERVICE." I am taken, by this gesture, aback. I run my fingers through front flaps, over pearled buttons, across soft cotton voids. This is no good—with the double-pronged tip of her carver, my Bernadette points to small curled hairs that lie upon her cutting board, hairs she accuses me of shedding. I shake plans of meadows, roaring fires, and beachside strolls. My Bernadette calls out, convincing the woman with the white shirt, black tie, and golden nameplate that reads "Pilar Poncé" to emerge from behind the cashier's register. Seeing the curled follicles, the Pilar insists I close my garment, that I hide what has become my ultimate shame. Compliance to her whim earns me a free pass to a lunch buffet, but in trade I have given up my Bernadette, banished to the kitchen, reappearing only to restock desserts, and worse, salad bar staples. The Pilar pierces the side of the lamb, slicing a thin, paltry cut, completing my journey without Bernadette's alluring smile to encourage a return.

My seat at the right hand of the buffet feels empty, as do my first-trip selections. The chickens' legs rest safely in crosses on my plate, loin juices have gelled into white grease, and even the measly slice of lamb lies gray, untasted. My last supper at this restaurant is cold, all except for the whole kernel corn, bellowing with the warmth of its juices. This corn is a step toward a new life. It is my corn; it is my diet. I will eat it in remembrance of an old me.

# THE BRAXTON-CARTER-VANDAMME-MYERS-BRAXTON-CARTER DIVORCE: AN OUTLINE

I. Characters

    A. Hal Braxton-Carter

        1. Husband: Wife, Miriam VanDamme-Myers-Braxton-Carter

        2. Father

            a) With Miriam VanDamme-Myers-Braxton-Carter: August Braxton-Carter-VanDamme-Myers, age 11; June Braxton-Carter-VanDamme-Myers, age 9; Sancho Braxton-Carter-VanDamme-Myers, age 2

            b) With Debbie Holstein: name undecided, age 7 months

        3. Historian

            a) Author

                (1) 13 journal articles, first author

                (2) 9 journal articles, various second through ninth author

                (3) 7 conference presentations

                (4) 2 poster presentations

                (5) novel, in progress

                (6) memoir, in progress

    b) Associate Professor: University of the Incarnate
       Word, relieved of duties

    c) Instructor: University of Phoenix, online

    d) Area of Specialization: Louisiana Purchase-
       era garb

  4. Fiancée: Debbie Holstein

  5. Amateur jazz drummer, inactive

B. Miriam VanDamme-Myers-Braxton-Carter

  1. Wife: Husband, Hal Braxton-Carter

  2. Mother: Children, August Braxton-Carter-
    VanDamme-Myers, age 11; June Braxton-Carter-
    VanDamme-Myers, age 9; Sancho Braxton-Carter-
    VanDamme-Myers, age 2

  3. Historian

    a) Author

      (1) 13 journal articles, first author

      (2) 9 journal articles, various second through
         ninth author

      (3) 11 conference presentations

      (4) 1 poster presentation

    b) Distinguished Professor: University of the
      Incarnate Word

    c) Area of Specialization: Louisiana Purchase-era
      feminism

  3. Girl Scout Leader

  4. City Council Member candidate

C. Debbie Holstein

  1. Student: University of the Incarnate Word, 7 credits
    shy, B.A. history

    a) Vice-President, History Club, relieved of duties

        b) Honorable Mention, Best Undergraduate Academic Paper, "A Intense Investigation Into the Functionality of Union Soldier Cuff Links, 1864-1865"

        c) Cashier, Culver's, present

        d) Reenactor, Docent: various, Alamo Tours, three summers, pending

    D. August Braxton-Carter-VanDamme-Myers

      1. Son, Hal Braxton-Carter and Miriam VanDamme-Myers-Braxton-Carter

      2. Teenager

II. Rising Action

    A. Hal Braxton-Carter publishes ninth first-author article, "The Coonskin Cap in Zeitgeist American Ideology," in esteemed history journal

    B. Dr. Emily Montenegro, Distinguished Professor of History, University of the Incarnate Word, dies suddenly, choking on chicken in chicken restaurant

    C. Research Assistantship opens for Hal Braxton-Carter

      1. Hal Braxton-Carter given freedom to choose assistant

      2. Debbie Holstein receives Honorable Mention for paper written in Hal Braxton-Carter's Advanced 18th-Century American History class

      3. Hal Braxton-Carter selects Debbie Holstein despite all top three finishers in history paper competition applying; all have higher GPA than Debbie, higher class standing, all male

      4. Debbie Holstein accepts assistantship, meets with Hal Braxton-Carter to arrange hours

D. Miriam VanDamme-Myers-Braxton-Carter receives haircut, dubs haircut "grown-up haircut," Hal Braxton-Carter expresses dislike

E. Miriam VanDamme-Myers-Braxton-Carter, in same conversation as haircut dislike conversation, reveals she has never cared for Hal Braxton-Carter's work, calls it "unnecessarily derivative and derivatively unnecessary"; imbibes several glasses of wine before and after statements

F. Hal Braxton-Carter retreats to campus office, bottle of wine in tow; finds Debbie Holstein organizing his belt buckle collection

G. Hal Braxton-Carter and Debbie Holstein start affair in office, on desk, amidst belt buckles

H. Miriam VanDamme-Myers-Braxton-Carter suspects immediately upon Hal Braxton-Carter's return, elaborate apology, and misbuttoned shirt; researches private investigators

III. Flashback

A. PhD-History candidate Miriam VanDamme-Myers meets PhD-History candidate Hal Braxton-Carter at history conference in Spokane, Washington

   1. Miriam VanDamme-Myers buys drink for Hal Braxton-Carter in La Quinta Inn bar, discusses dissertation topic

   2. Hal Braxton-Carter invites Miriam VanDamme-Myers to room where the two proceed to finish drinks, have intercourse, exchange contact information

B. Miriam VanDamme-Myers and Hal Braxton-Carter receive PhDs at same time, apply for same jobs, Hal

Braxton-Carter receiving only offer, University of Incarnate Word, Miriam VanDamme-Myers accepting adjunct position at same school (promoted to tenure-track two years later)

C. Miriam VanDamme-Myers marries Hal Braxton-Carter and becomes Miriam VanDamme-Myers-Braxton-Carter, each pledging eternal love and devotion

IV. Rising Action Resumes

A. Hal Braxton-Carter acts rejuvenated in home. Takes larger interest in children, wife, though not sexually (wife)

B. Hal Braxton-Carter often forgets important papers at office, necessitating return trips late at night.

C. Hal Braxton-Carter has heart-to-heart discussion with August VanDamme-Myers-Braxton-Carter about sex

  1. Graphic illustrations helpful but inappropriate

  2. August VanDamme-Myers-Braxton-Carter reveals crush on Debbie Holstein, father's research assistant, says he thinks about her boobs in the shower, at school, while riding bike

  3. Father-son discussion on sex; August VanDamme-Myers-Braxton-Carter now allowed to watch R-rated movies, begins with *Something Wild* starring Melanie Griffith

D. Miriam VanDamme-Myers-Braxton-Carter congratulates Hal Braxton-Carter on fathering accomplishments, asks to keep Debbie Holstein away from house, away from August VanDamme-Myers-Braxton-Carter

  1. Rewards Hal Braxton-Carter with sex

  2. Notes changes in Hal Braxton-Carter's demeanor during

a) Is more aggressive
b) Suggests new positions
    (1) sitting, living room couch, both facing (and watching) television
    (2) standing, Miriam VanDamme-Myers-Braxton-Carter's hands pressed against wall; position interrupted, Miriam VanDamme-Myers-Braxton-Carter unable to spread legs at appropriate angle
    (3) missionary, eyes closed
c) Is later than usual in announcing he's forgotten papers at office

V. Climax

A. Miriam VanDamme-Myers-Braxton-Carter returns early from conference, finds Hal Braxton-Carter in marital bedroom engaged in sex with Debbie Holstein, standing, Debbie Holstein's hands pressed up against wall
    1. Miriam VanDamme-Myers-Braxton-Carter vows violence against Hal Braxton-Carter, disregards Debbie Holstein
    2. Pregnancy of Debbie Holstein revealed by Debbie Holstein
    3. Pregnancy of Debbie Holstein officially last for Hal Braxton-Carter, Miriam VanDamme-Myers rendering him unable to reproduce again
    4. Exchange of detrimental and damaging passages
        a) Miriam VanDamme-Myers-Braxton-Carter (to Hal Braxton-Carter): "Nobody cares about belt buckles. Or shoelaces. Or socks. You have wasted

your life and the lives of everyone who has ever read a word of your research"

  b) Hal Braxton-Carter (to Miriam VanDamme-Myers): "Sacagawea was not a real person."

  c) Debbie Holston (to Miriam VanDamme-Myers): "You have the same hair as my grandma"

  d) Miriam VanDamme-Myers-Braxton-Carter (to Debbie Holstein):

   "Whore"

    (1) "Fucking slut-can whore."

    (2) "Fucking slut-can, big-thighed, brainless, home-wrecking, flexible whore"

 5. Unoffically, Miriam VanDamme-Myers-Braxton-Carter becomes Miriam VanDamme-Myers; official change pending

VI. Resolution

 A. Miriam VanDamme-Myers promoted to Full Professor, takes children, August Braxton-Carter-VanDamme-Myers, June VanDamme-Myers, and Sancho VanDamme-Myers, on year-long research expedition, following exact path of Lewis, Clark, and Sacagawea, publishes paper, makes Distinguished Professor

 B. Hal Braxton-Carter weds Debbie Holstein two weeks before Grant Lee Holstein-Braxton-Carter born; couple moves to Debbie Holstein's on-campus apartment; Hal Braxton-Carter denied promotion to Full Professor by peers, asked to leave university

  1. August Braxton-Carter-VanDamme-Myers only child to visit

    2. Is not asked to leave room when Debbie Holstein-
       Braxton-Carter feeds Grant Lee Holstein-
       Braxton-Carter

C. Epiphany: Hal Braxton-Carter remembers passage
  from Lewis and Clark journals, where Clark, convinced
  he was shooting at an elk, shoots Lewis in the leg instead,
  wounding but not killing him:

    1. Hal Braxton-Carter likens this situation to his own,
       comparing himself, then Debbie, to Lewis

       a) Considers theme of identity

       b) Identifies himself as victim and hero

    2. Audience does or does not make connection

# HOT LETTUCE

Thourgar the Castrator commands me to blow him in the backstage bathroom during intermission. I remind him that I sing the first song of the encore and I need my mouth for other things. He kisses me on the forehead, smudging my makeup, and reminds me that dozens of groupies in the crowd would murder their parents for the opportunity.

A stage tech from the club taps Thourgar on the shoulder and Thourgar goes ballistic, grabbing the stage tech by his crotch. Just in time, Kip, a.k.a. Güdalla the Pulverizer, starts bashing his cymbals, propelling Thourgar to his place on stage, the techie left fetal like a pill bug on the floor. I apologize, then I launch myself to my mark, reaching the mic just in time to scream,

> *I've got a fever in my heaving chest*
> *You've got what I need, cleaving the rest*
> *Shove your meat stick down my throat*
> *Gauge the fire, make me choke*

The crowd goes apeshit. "Throat Thermometer" is technically our biggest hit, once No. 1 in Denmark two weeks in a row. Several boys in the crowd thrust their groins in my direction. Without fail, one kid pulls his dick out of his skinny jeans and shows it to me, prompting a security guard to drag him out. Thourgar shreds and Güdalla bashes and Larry, a.k.a. Demonico the Defibulator, bangs his head against his keyboard (which, unknown to Hot Lettuce Nation, isn't plugged in—Demonico can't play a lick). All eyes are on me, my one vocal, a few of those eyes not on my tits. For a few minutes, I remember how much I love this and just wail.

After the show, the rest of us tear down and load the tour bus while Thourgar entertains a bevy of mascara-stained trollops. Thourgar invites me to join in, but I opt to get gyros with Kip and Larry at the Greek joint across from the club. We are in Normal, Illinois, I think, but it could be Champaign or Peoria—the tour's been that long. Kip says I sounded good today and I tell him he sounded good, too. Larry has tzatziki on his face and is staring out at the bus; Thourgar won't allow him into orgies until he learns to play. You'd think this would be incentive enough, but Larry has fingers like smoky links and is tone deaf. Brain damage looms like a sunrise.

A few Hot Lettuce fans come in for spanakopita and sit one table over. For a second, I think a kid with Thorgour makeup makes us, but Kip's telling a story about his twin girls starting lacrosse on Saturday. The kid hears this and makes a comment about us being dinosaurs, quoting our song "Feast on Grandma": *May her meat sustain you/let your inheritance entertain you.*

Outside, every ten minutes, a girl, sometimes two, steps off our bus, straightening her skirt, stilettos under her arms, fishnets tip-toeing the pavement. I ask Kip how long we give Thourgar and he says we should just go in when we're ready. Crossing Indiana always takes longer than we think. We throw our garbage away and Larry buys a chicken pita combo for

Thourgar. On our way out, one of our fanboys throws half a shake at Kip's back and Kip trudges out as it seeps down his T-shirt.

Inside the bus, Thourgar is not happy to see us, especially after I refuse to help him undress the remaining sluts.

"Who're these bagels?" one slut says, "bagels" being Hot Lettucese for Kip and Larry's doughy roundness. She has green hair and a tattoo of my made-up face in her cleavage. "The bus drivers?"

I tell the girls they can either get off the bus now or they hitchhike home when we stop for gas. They all opt to stay. We'll be in Indianapolis by the time we stop, and I'm starting to think some of these girls aren't over eighteen. I get Kip to back me and Thourgar throws a fit, but then sees Larry fingering the pita. We refuse to give him the combo until the girls leave.

"Does it have lettuce?" Thourgar asks. Lettuce on a hot sandwich that gets squishy, almost a liquid, is what Thourgar calls the world's greatest evil. It's how he named the band: He couldn't think of anything worse on Earth than hot lettuce.

"No hot lettuce," I say.

Thourgar relents, but not before one of the girls pops a tit from her bustier and asks Thourgar to Castrate her—in Hot Lettuce speak, "Castrate" means bite her, hard enough to leave a mark, to make her bleed, the greatest honor in our fandom. We turn our heads as Thourgar completes the task to the enthralled screams of the teen.

"Where to next?" Thourgar says, the four of us now alone. "Madison Square Garden? Wembley? The Coliseum?"

"Dayton," I say.

"Outstanding," Thourgar declares. He informs me he'd love a hummer after he eats, or, if I don't mind, while.

I don't respond, heading up front to keep Kip company. Larry stays with Thourgar to renegotiate his orgy dibs. Thourgar throws a tantrum because we forgot ketchup for his fries.

"Two more shows," I say to Kip. He nods and turns on a country station for the drive.

Before Thourgar became the Castrator, he was Allen Gannon and he worked with me and Kip at Circuit City. Allen was a floor salesman, Kip repaired computers, and I did customer service. As the store was going belly-up, we spent a lot of time doing inventory in the back. This is where Allen first unveiled his plan for Hot Lettuce. He played guitar and Kip played drums, and because I was a woman, he said I could be the bassist. I couldn't play, but it all seemed like fun, something we could do at local bars. That wasn't what Allen had in mind. When he brought his Stratocaster to work and started playing, we knew: Allen wasn't a townie guitarist. He sucked at selling stereos, lived in his Buick LeSabre, and hadn't been to a dentist since birth. But he was a genius, a flat-out *genius* at guitar, the best either of us had ever seen.

"What kind of music do you want to play?" I asked. I'd been listening to Cool and the Gang, Pearl Jam, Shania Twain, and Drake on the we-play-everything station in my car. This either prepared me for anything or meant I wasn't hardcore. I was betting on the latter.

Allen unfolded a piece of paper from his pocket. On it were doodles, in crayon, of crazy goth demons with wings and chains and horns and Halloween makeup, blood spraying from every orifice, musical instruments in their hands.

Allen pointed to the paper: "Whatever type of music this is."

Fifty miles outside Dayton, Thourgar awakens, demanding waffles and women. Thourgar occupies the large compartment in the back, where he entertains, eats libido-sustaining food, and composes impossible guitar licks. The rest of us sleep in bunk beds in a smaller compartment, though Kip and I always drive all night, taking turns dozing in the passenger seat. Larry often sees double—triple under a full moon. It's understood that Larry doesn't drive.

Kip offers to find a Waffle House, which Thourgar hates: "Subpar pussy," he says. I vote that we get to the gig, unload our gear, maybe relax before the show.

"You'll sleep in your coffin," Thourgar says, which is either a vague threat or a fact: Our bunk beds were built to look like coffins.

Thourgar spots an IHOP at the next exit and insists upon stopping. He likes their flavored syrups and brand of ass. Unlike the rest of us, Thourgar refuses to be seen in public out of character, meaning that if we get off the bus, which reads "Hot Lettuce" on the side in bleeding script, he has to be in full make-up and costume. That means we have to be in full costume. Early on, we acquiesced, putting that shit on two or three times a day, even to stop for gas. Now, three albums and five tours later, we just want to eat bacon without spikes shooting from our shoulder pads. Thourgar descends on the IHOP, the rest of us opting for granola bars.

"We should drive off," Kip suggests. He does this this every time Thourgar steps out.

"Two more shows," I remind Kip.

After Circuit City closed, we practiced ten hours a day. I got good enough to keep time with Kip, but really, my job was to have large breasts and jump up and down, which I'd aced from day one. We went through keyboardists like hairspray. Allen said he could play keyboards on the album—genius at those, too—then teach our songs to a touring member. He recruited Larry, his parents' accountant, because Larry was pale, had beady black eyes, and wore a spiked cock ring in his everyday life—we to this day don't know why Allen knew that. After a few weeks, songs emerged. Then gigs. Within a year we had a following. Six months later, a record deal. Twelve- to nineteen-year-old-boys adored us, twelve-to-sixty-year-old women lusted after Thourgar. That's when Allen disappeared—we were no longer allowed to speak that name.

As this was happening, Allen and I were fucking. Before the band began, I'd already had my eye on him, tall and confident, always sending customers my way. Then I saw him play guitar and I wanted him: the way his fingers moved across the strings made me wonder what they could do to me. The day we first saw him play, Allen took me way back in the warehouse and we did it three times on a stack of washing machines. Allen knew what he was doing. He also had a giant porn cock. On top of those washers, I felt like I was going places.

The fact I was a burgeoning death metal star fell through the cracks with my parents. My mom worked at the Fifth/Third Bank across the street, and even when the Circuit City became a Big Lots, she never asked where I went all day. I was nineteen, out of work over a year, mooching off them, yet no questions. When we signed the record deal and I got my share of the advance, twenty-five grand, they didn't understand. I told them I was leaving home for eight months, headed across the U.S., Canada, and Korea. We were big in Korea. They forbade me to go.

"No daughter of mine is going to be a rock star," Mom said.

"Which Korea?" Dad asked.

"South," I said.

"We should let her go, Jean."

Kip's wife wasn't thrilled, either, especially when she saw me in a tube top. Thourgar assured her that I was *his* bitch, that I would want nothing to do with some paltry drummer while he was around. To ensure Kip could go, Thourgar, right in front of Kip, his wife, and the newly hired Larry, popped out my left boob and performed the very first Hot Lettuce Castration. It hurt like a motherfo, but we needed Kip. I clenched my teeth and took it for the team.

"OK, fine. Go," Kip's wife said. She looked like she wanted to vomit.

The IHOP waitress Thourgar sullies stays on the bus to Dayton. She is not underage and is there of her own volition, so no objections from me or Kip.

"Wow," Kip says when she emerges to use the head.

"What?" I say.

"She's stacked."

"I didn't notice," I lie. The waitress, since halfway across the IHOP parking lot, has been naked.

"Only woman I've seen more stacked than you."

"It was inevitable," I say. Eight years ago, I would have ripped my shirt off just to prove Kip wrong. Today, I'm more upset that Kip felt the need to point it out. Not once has he made a move on me, or any groupie, in all our years on the road. I cut him some slack.

"I bet she can't play bass," I say.

We've played the Victoria Theater on Dayton's riverfront before. They have men to unload our gear, which is why it's one of my favorite venues. As a kicker, they have mind-blowing acoustics. Hot Lettuce sounds good in Dayton. I sound good in Dayton. Dayton doesn't injure my lower back.

The in-house roadies unload and set us up, giving us rare free time. I consider a nap in my coffin, which I've slept in fewer than ten times. I could have my nails done, my *actual* nails. I could get a massage. Dayton isn't the spa capital of North America, but Daytonites or Daytonians or whatever they're called must spoil themselves, too.

While Kip calls Alison and Larry sits outside Thourgar's chamber, his ear pressed to the door, I wander off toward the river. I don't find any salons or boutiques or even cafes. A rat climbs out of the water, snoops around, dives back in. I spy a hot dog vendor, a guy selling ice cream, and a mime. He's badgering a woman with three kids, a woman who wants him to leave her alone. I wonder if the mime does his own makeup. His base is flawless.

I head back toward the theater, but stop at a record store I passed on my way. I haven't been in a record store, save promotions and live feeds, since before HL. Even then, I bought CDs at Circuit City with my discount. I don't even have copies of the Hot Lettuce albums.

This store seems to be doing its best to hold on, selling rarities, imports, and vinyl, pushing local bands, covering its walls with posters, flats, and T-shirts. A Hot Lettuce broadside from Whiskey-a-Go-Go hangs in one corner, though half of it's covered by a Vampire Weekend poster. It's another reason I'd love to hang those dickless twerps by their deck shoes.

I flip through the racks, checking to see how much Hot Lettuce they have, noting three copies of our latest plus one of our debut. I consider buying one, sliding it into the CD deck when Kip is sleeping, see how long it takes him to wake up. A gag not worth $15.95, I decide, and head to the door.

"Good luck tonight," I hear. I stop.

The guy behind the counter, forty if not fifty, waves.

"I'm going," he says. "I've seen you guys eight times. I drove to Toledo once. Toledo sucks."

I can't think of anything to say to get me off the hook.

"You're Tigressa," he says.

"Thanks," I say. I think of what Thourgar has said about being out sans costume. Then I think, *Two more shows.* I say to myself, *Fuck Thourgar.*

The guy's name is Dick and he's the owner. He admits he loses money hand over fist, but he made a mint in real estate and now just listens to records and gets high all day. He says it's his dream come true.

"That is, until you walked in."

I sign every piece of memorabilia Dick has in his store, plus wait till he runs up to his apartment—he owns the building—to get all his Hot Lettuce ticket stubs, T-shirts, and the foam poleax from our *Flay the U.S.A.* tour.

I spend my entire two hours of down time with Dick. He has a lot of questions, secrets I'm not supposed to reveal but do, some of them stupid—"No, Dick, Thourgar's penis is not JFK reborn"—and some of them realistic—"We split the money four ways, but I'm pretty sure Demonico gets less." Dick is fascinated. He asks if we have to supply our own fake blood (we do, but I insist it's not fake) and if Kip's tail is real (it's not, but I say it is). Dick talks about my playing, tells me I'm good, not as good as Thourgar, but good. He read my interview in *Bassist* magazine and took up bass right then and there. He can play most of our songs, though he needs the sheet music, which I didn't know existed.

On my way out—curtain in an hour and me looking like a soccer mom—I tell Dick I'll look for him at the show, look his way when I sing "Throat Thermometer."

"You should just do it now," Dick says.

"I don't want to lose my voice," I say, thinking Dick is asking me to sing.

"Not that." Suddenly, the blinds of the store are shutting by themselves and the lights are dimming. Dick is pressing buttons on a tiny remote control. When it's mostly dark, he undoes his pants.

"What the fuck?" I say.

"You know," he repeats.

"No, I don't."

"You're sex mistress to Thourgar the Castrator and his minions, Güdalla the Pulverizer and Demonico the Defibulator. You relieve them of purity and spray their seed across the universe so the gods will keep them rocking for ten thousand years."

Dick is quoting the copy on the back of our first album cover, declaring me divine bassist and concubine of Hot Lettuce and all its fans. I back toward the door and turn the handle, hoping Dick's remote can't lock me inside. Dick's too busy stroking his bushwad and I'm able to slip out. As I flee, I hear Dick outside yelling, "Purify me!" I turn around and see him putting his dick away, the mime from the riverfront standing behind him, making the same motion.

I have forty minutes to get dressed, do makeup, and study the set list. Kip, in Güdalla garb, stops me at the door, says we have to talk, but I push through, noting the time. I search our dressing area for my things, but can't find them. I look at Kip.

"He dressed the IHOP waitress in your shit. He's teaching her how to fake-play backstage right now."

I march to the backstage door, where a huge mountain of steroid blocks my path.

"I'm in the band," I say. "I'm Tigressa."

"Tigressa went inside twenty minutes ago," the mountain says. "She's a fake."

"You should beat it," the man says. When he puts his hand on my shoulder, I jettison my foot into his junk. The door behind him isn't locked.

Backstage, Thourgar—check that, *Allen*—is standing behind the IHOP whore, his arms stretched over her shoulders, moving her bird claws across my bass neck. She is wearing my clothes, my wig, my armor, and my make-up. None of that matters—she can keep the get-up—but playing my bass? Uh-uh.

Before Allen can react, I pick up Larry's keyboard and swing it, hoping to catch Allen under the jaw. Instead, I hit the IHOP whore in the cheekbone, eliciting a loud crack. She hits the floor. Allen drops to his knees, begs me not to hurt him.

I raise the keyboard over my head, lining it up with Allen's skull. Years of bullshit bum-rush my brain. Allen doing interviews by himself. How he's never once helped us load or unload the bus, or let us hire roadies or drivers. Allen telling Kip and Larry about having sex with me. Allen telling our fans about sex with me. Him cheating on me after our first show. Allen asking for it years after we broke up. Me only singing one song. The stupid lyrics. The stupid costumes. The piercings. Tattoos. The clap. All this makes me thrust the keyboard downward.

"That's mine," Larry says, grabbing his deck before I make contact with Allen's skull. "Plus, don't kill Thourgar. You'd go to jail."

Allen remains on his knees. A puddle of stink has pooled between his legs. The security and theater personnel stare with their mouths agape. Kip walks in and sees Allen and the waitress.

"I quit," I say.

"Me, too," Kip says.

Kip peels off his armor, uses his cape to wipe his face clean. He reaches for his tail, then leaves it on.

"I like the tail," he says.

I remove my bass from the out-cold whore's shoulder. Kip eyes his drums and asks some of the stage guys to help him break down. This confirms the gig is canceled.

Allen begs us not to go, reminds us there's just two more shows. He says he'll sue. He says he'll replace us. We ignore him. He pleads with Larry to talk us into staying, offering Larry at least one groupie per night. Larry looks to me, sees it's a definitive no, and starts to cry.

With the bus loaded, we tell Allen and Larry they can come with us or stay here. Allen claims we can't take the bus and we remind him it's half ours, that Kip has the keys. Larry wants a ride back to Hershey. Allen opts to stay behind. He declares that Thourgar will rise and see all our souls tortured for our betrayal.

In the same breath, he asks me for a blowjob. "One for old time's sake?"

I stop Kip from defending me—he's about to charge. I tell him I have this. I instruct Thourgar to lean against the wall and relax.

"Really?" he says.

"Really?" Kip says.

"Really," I say.

I strip off Allen's kneepads, work his leather chaps down his waxed thighs, and kneel down. Everyone is watching, Kip, Larry, the waitress with the busted face, all the Victoria employees.

"Ready?" I say. I release Allen's dick from its crimson thong.

"Ready."

Allen closes his eyes, waiting for me to start, his head shifted to the side as if trying to align with the stars. He begins thrusting in my hands. He says he loves me, which he says to everyone in my position. Best of all, he is unaware he's about to receive the first-ever Hot Lettuce Male Castration.

# YOU HAD ME AT ZOO

Conner's first-ever blind date is at the zoo. He meets Melanie at the gate, where she buys both tickets, plus passes for the amphitheater, dolphin show, and train ride. She also springs for meal coupons and a fifty-dollar certificate for the gift shop. She tells Conner that she used to work there and still has her discount card, so it's all on her.

"Too bad you didn't work at a bank," Conner says. Melanie doesn't laugh.

Conner follows Melanie to the flamingo pond, where she points to each bird, reciting its name, temperament, with whom it likes to mate. There must be fifty flamingos. Conner is impressed and wonders why she quit. He can't imagine being so involved in something and walking away.

Conner hasn't visited a zoo since he was a kid, but remembers disliking them. The heat. The stink. The animals just sleeping. On a field trip, a sheep bit his classmate and swallowed her fingertip. There was a lot of blood, on Brandy Frederick and on the sheep.

Melanie doesn't only know flamingos. She knows every animal, the camels, kangaroos, wildebeests, zebras, all the reptiles and big cats. Stories begin to accompany facts. Melanie once pulled a lion's tooth. Another time, a colobus monkey stole her belt buckle, making her pants fall in front of a tour. A penguin crawled into her backpack and she didn't find it until she got home. Just recently, she delivered a grizzly bear cub, which the zoo named after her and she considered her baby. She emphasizes: *"Mine."* Conner begins questioning her authenticity. Why would a flamingo expert be asked to pull lion teeth? Conner suspects that all these things happened, just not to Melanie.

At noon, Melanie announces the halfway point. Conner predicts her intentions, to visit every animal, plus do the shows and train ride. When Melanie suggests lunch at the cafeteria, shaped like a giant birdcage, Conner decides to leave afterward. Melanie is attractive, pleasant, and clearly intelligent, but Conner senses bad instincts. He can't imagine where this goes from here. He pictures sex, her illustrating each body part: "My vagina once escaped my pants and was taken down with a tranquilizer gun."

Melanie tells Conner to find a table and insists on ordering the food. She returns with large bags, nothing on trays, nothing to drink. Conner thinks Melanie wants to leave, too, that she realizes what she's done and is trying to rescue the date. It might be too late, but he is hungry, so he gives it lunch to decide.

Melanie walks out of the cafe and Conner follows, asking what's in the bags. For the first time, Melanie is silent. She walks with determination, almost as if she's trying to lose him. She is headed toward the ape house.

"We eating in there?" Conner asks. "Is it air conditioned?"

"Wait here," Melanie commands, taking the food with her.

Within seconds, Conner hears a piercing siren, a fire alarm. Melanie emerges with all the other visitors.

"I guess we can't eat in there," Conner says.

"Guess not," Melanie says.

Melanie again soldiers forward, heading toward the aviary. Conner sees the front gate just over a hill, knows he could ditch her, be in the lot before she notices him gone. When Melanie enters the building, Conner jogs toward his car.

Conner stops, however, when he hears another fire alarm. He hates to, but he turns and sees people coming out of the aviary. Melanie is headed right for him. Conner has a bad feeling.

"It's important that you keep up now," she says. She reaches into a bag and tosses him a hamburger. "In case you're hungry."

A fire truck arrives, as well as several police cars. Zoo security ushers the uniforms past Melanie and Conner on the path. Conner can cut and run at any time, but something about Melanie compels him to follow her. He wants to know where this is going. He unwraps his burger, takes a bite, lags behind.

Melanie enters the North America exhibit. They pass gray wolves, a beaver pond, a prairie dog town. Several of the varmints peek from their holes and Conner winks at them as he passes. Zoo visitors head in the other direction, toward all the alarms, curious. Conner wonders about the animals, what all the noise must do to their ears.

Bear Country looms at exhibit's end. Melanie yells back that this is where she worked. They have black bears, brown bears, a bunch of grizzlies. Conner asks about polar bears and Melanie explains those are in the Arctic exhibit. She adds, "Duh." Conner does not inquire about koalas or pandas.

Melanie passes the black bears, sleeping on rocks; the brown bears do the same. Last come the grizzlies, where Melanie stops.

"That's Hondo," she says, pointing at the largest bear slumbering on top of a rock formation.

"Would he remember you?" Conner asks.

"Of course," Melanie says, then runs through the names and habits of them all, including the cub she helped birth, Mel, asleep under its mother's paw.

Before Conner can catch sight of the baby, Melanie instructs him to watch for people on the path, particularly zoo employees. If he sees one, he is to ask about the fire alarms, ask as many questions as possible. Melanie unbuttons her blouse and pulls a large gym bag from her pants. She is much thinner than Conner had thought.

Conner inspects the gym bag, filled with blankets, watching as Melanie throws the four bags of hamburgers into the grizzly pit, distributing them to the far corners of the cave. *Don't feed the bears*, Conner mouths. Melanie says it back, mocking him: "That's right! Don't feed the bears!"

Melanie climbs atop the railing, the gym bag under her arm, balancing herself like a gymnast. Conner stares as she backflips down, then runs to look over the side.

# KULKULKAN

Today, some guy at the P.O. mistook me for an employee and handed me a box. I stood by the counter, a bin of my own mail in hand, the only clerk fetching more of my mail from the back. The box the guy handed to me was cube-shaped, its size and weight making me think bowling ball. "It's all ready," he said, and left; a label for $58.04 resided in the proper corner. The clerk reemerged with a second bin of catalogues, flyers, and bills, looked at the box, asked, "That for me?" I declined. What if it was a bomb? Like at the airport, if you accept a stranger's parcel and it's a bomb, you're an accomplice. I considered the box now mine—nine-tenths, et cetera—and threw it atop my backlog.

I hadn't been out of town. My wife'd left me for a workplace dullard, a director, she claimed, though he still worked at the pet store, cleaning shit and shilling seed. They were wintering in Greece on some kind of fellowship he'd won. She'd return in the spring for her things and settle matters with lawyers; she said I could have everything. My plan? Kill myself, as soon as possible and give my body time to decompose to the point she'll need to get in close to identify me. To ensure she'd find me, not some cop on a tip, I wiped myself from the grid. I quit my job, used our savings to pay the bills six months ahead. I canceled the cable and newspaper and halted the mail. Out front I erected a sign—

NO TRESPASSING—and adhered others—NO SOLICITORS—to each door. A privacy fence fortified top-notch security. The only person who'd have reason to approach our house was Wendy, overtanned and overfucked from Greece. With her in mind, I envisioned a hanging. I constructed a note and dashed out a will, leaving everything to Derek Ahlberg, the artiste she now loved. Unquestionably, I would be nude.

Home from the P.O., I cleared the table of dishes, rotting food, and dirty clothes. I set up extra lights and washed my hands. I searched for a box cutter, the entire package lathered in tape, settling on a Ginsu. As I sawed through the tape on the box the guy had handed me, I read the name in the middle of the top flap: The box was addressed to my wife, in Greece. An incredible coincidence. Then I wondered: Was it on purpose? Maybe the guy and I had known each other and when he saw me, assumed I'd give the box to my wife. But what would a stranger, a fourth party, need to mail her? All her precious belongings were here— her grandmother's China, family photo albums, the stuffed parrot, Filbert. She was holidaying on an affair. Why would she need something so heavy? I was suddenly terrified of what the box held. I dropped the knife, excommunicating the box to the attic. It wasn't mine. It might have been a bomb. Nothing good could be in the box.

I bought a rope, removed the ceiling fan from our bedroom ceiling, and tied a noose to the fixture, allowing room for dangle. I cleaned the house and made the bed. I turned off the thermostat and unplugged every appliance. Potpourri graced every room. Five times I climbed a chair. Twice I encircled my neck with the noose. I couldn't jump either time. Days passed, then weeks. The noose lingered above our bed while I slept, the end tickling my hips if I tossed or turned. I reordered cable. I craved Chinese food, eating it daily. I gained weight, my beard as long as my neck. I scattered both mail bins in the foyer and welcomed insects and rodents. My reimagined plan: Instead of a controlled suicide, I would let myself go. Seeing me deteriorated would make Wendy feel worse. The old plan depicted me as insane, her leaving me justified. This new plan—me pathetic but still dead—was a solid rewrite. I could wait to kill myself until she pulled in the driveway. I'd eke a last twitch as her eyes met mine.

For our fifth anniversary, eight years before Greece, we'd vacationed in Chichen Itza. We arrived in Cancun and were bused to the site, where we stayed at a hotel. When Wendy went to bed, I paid our guide nearly a month's salary to arrange a surprise my wife would savor. At dawn, the guide took us straight to the top of the main pyramid, the Temple of Kukulkan. Waiting for us was an altar, decked out with a tablecloth, candles, crystal ware, a fabulous spread. We feasted and drank wine, a violinist plucked romance, then we ate a dessert too rich to enjoy. Busloads of hot tourists clamored at ground level. When our time ended, the guide offered me a brick the size of a mailbox, a piece of the actual temple, a piece we could take home. It was priceless. Still, I wanted to leave it—there was no way they'd let us board the plane with a piece of their national treasure—but Wendy insisted. I carried the brick all day, held it on my lap on the bus back to Cancun. The day we checked out, I left the brick on the desk for housekeeping, along with five dollars and some Mexican coins. Back at home, my wife asked me for the brick, and when I told her I'd abandoned it, she was furious. She called the hotel concierge, giving our room number and the day we checked out. I doubted her pursuit, but sure enough, the concierge said he could find it, told her not to worry. I apologized, explaining my customs fears. She replied, "That brick was mine. I told you I needed that. They're sending it to me tomorrow."

# SPACE

When Miller's wife went up into space, he set out to cheat on her. The day after liftoff, he met a woman at an Olive Garden bar an hour north and bought her a drink at last call. The woman left her car in the Walmart lot across the street and drove home with Miller, her hand in his lap and tongue in his ear the entire way to Cape Canaveral. Miller hadn't picked up a woman in fifteen years, not since Meg, not that he'd ever picked up Meg—they were in classes together at Carnegie Mellon and were married Thanksgiving break, senior year. He didn't even remember asking her out.

This Olive Garden woman, on him like an envelope, had fallen for a line: "Last call at my apartment isn't until sunrise." She'd downed her whiskey sour and said, "Lead the way." The whole drive, Miller had to shake loose his right arm so he could shift. With five drinks in him and one eye on the stars, they were lucky to stay on the road.

Miller pulled up to the base and remembered the checkpoint. He'd forgotten about the MPs who had to wave him on, who had to inspect all vehicles, check in all visitors. He'd lived on the base for two years and the regular guys knew his Outback, knew him by face. They also knew Meg and where she was, that this drunk, horny woman wasn't her. Miller wanted to turn around, find a motel up the coast, what he should have done, anyway, but then another car and an Army transport pulled behind him. Miller decided the woman, who was fading, would be his sister, or better yet, Meg's sister, in for the launch. There'd be the record of the lie, but it wasn't like Meg was going to check. As long as the MP at the gate wouldn't say something like, "It was nice meeting your sister!" when Meg got back, Miller would be fine.

Miller enjoyed the sex with the woman, whose name, unbelievably, was Venus Armstrong. Out of her clothes, Venus acted with even more confidence, unlike Miller, who had to be forced out of everything, even his socks. Miller later speculated that Venus had had more of these encounters than he. Maybe his line wasn't as great as he'd thought. He congratulated himself for insisting on condoms, though he worried a corner of the foil wrapper would one day, maybe years from now, show up when Meg moved the nightstand to vacuum.

When Miller and Venus settled down—they had gone three rounds, a personal record for Miller by two rounds—the woman wanted to know what he did at the base, if he was important. In other words, was he was an astronaut. Miller wanted to put his clothes back on for this part of the encounter, Venus in his arms, in his marital bed, everything so personal all of a sudden. He fought the urge: Astronauts didn't get out of bed with women to put on pajamas. In fact, astronauts didn't wear pajamas, not even Meg, who wore panties and a nightshirt. Miller noticed he was overthinking: They'd already had the sex. He needed to relax.

In answering Venus' question, he went for it. "I'm an astronaut. A pilot, one of three living shuttle jockeys in the western hemisphere. Two are up in space as of 0500 hours yesterday, and then there's me." Venus wanted to know why he wasn't up in space—of course she did—and Miller was ready with an answer he'd thought of on his way to the Olive Garden: "They rotate us. I went the last two times, so this was my turn to stay here. Someone's got to be able to fly the rescue shuttle in case the astronauts up there need help."

"Wow," Venus said, and Miller thought she might want to have more sex. Just as he was about to explain what it was like to break through the atmosphere at 25,000 miles an hour, Venus fell asleep on his arm, her head making his biceps go pins and needles. After a while of hoping she'd roll over, Miller pulled out from under Venus and went out to the couch, drifting off after a couple of hours of not being able to.

Miller and Meg both applied to join the astronaut corps while finishing their PhDs in Engineering at MIT. They were recent newlyweds, but took the chance anyway, since the current selection cycle was their best opportunity. Both were accepted into the two-year training program, both enlisted, and both succeeded in surviving their candidate class. Eventually, they realized that any particular mission only needed one engineer, so their dream of going up together, the first husband and wife team in space, wasn't likely. Still, they turned heads, and figured each of them would get a shot.

When final selection time came, Meg stood head and shoulders above Miller in every category, her body sturdier for the rigors of space travel. Both of them were whizzes with the science, Miller perhaps a shade sharper, but during their last simulation, Miller threw up inside his suit for the umpteenth time, sealing his fate as a "manager astronaut." Miller would work on the base and in mission control, but NASA didn't blast off people who yacked in their masks.

NASA called Meg at their house three days later, Miller

outside watering the garden. Miller heard Meg's phone ring and moved next to the kitchen window where Meg was standing. Meg screamed, jumped up and down, and Miller knew: She had orders. Miller dropped his hose, still spewing water, pumping his fist. He wouldn't going into space, but his wife, his friend, and his life companion, would. Miller couldn't be happier for her, and really, after that last simulation, his guts spinning and his nerves failing, Miller felt relieved. The only thing that scared him about space was getting to and from space, so he was content to stay on the ground and cheer for his wife, who seemed destined for this very adventure.

Before Miller went inside to congratulate Meg, he heard more of her conversation, heard her repeating the details; then laughing. "No, he'll get over it," she said. "He might throw up again, but that's just what he does." Miller stopped listening to the conversation and jogged to the other side of the yard to resume watering. When Meg came outside with her news, Miller feigned surprise, lifting her up in the air, twirling her around. He kept her up there for a long time, just staring at her above him. He said, "I can't wait for you to go. It's going to be awesome."

Miller woke on the couch with his laptop buzzing next to his head. He saw the microwave clock in the kitchen and realized he'd slept until 11 a.m. Meg was supposed to Skype him at 11. She was Skyping him now. From space.

"Is there a connection problem there?" Meg said when she appeared on Miller's screen. "You know I don't have all day."

Miller almost said that he'd forgotten.

"The wireless is slow. It was slow yesterday, too."

"Did you just get up?" Meg said. "And why are you naked?"

Miller knew what this must look like, mainly because it was what it looked like.

"How's space?" he said. "It's got to be amazing."

"Pretty amazing," Meg said. "And vast."

Miller saw her heels floating above her head behind her. "Tell me all about it. I want to know everything. The weightlessness. The launch. Did you want to throw up?"

Miller wished he hadn't asked that last question.

"I don't have time for all that. We get ten minutes every other day. It's not like on TV, just Skyping and singing David Bowie."

"Pick one," Miller said. He wanted to look at the bedroom door, to see if it was shut, if Venus was still there. He denied the urge. "What's weightlessness like?"

"Miller," Meg said. "Who was that woman you brought home last night?"

Miller stared at the screen.

"You know, we have machines up here that can see down there."

"What woman?" Miller still said.

"Miller, don't. When we got here, the Russians were showing me around and asked what I wanted to see. Someone joked, 'I can see my house from here,' so I asked to see my house.

"I saw you pull up with a woman. I saw her all over you."

Miller heard urine hitting water in their bedroom bathroom. He reached to turn the volume down on the laptop. He whispered, "That wasn't me."

"Miller, they use this equipment to detect dark matter. I saw you bring a woman home last night. All the other astronauts saw it, too. Even the Russians saw you with her."

Before Miller could say anything else, Venus walked out of the bedroom, right through the line of the laptop camera's sight.

Like Miller, she was still naked. Upright and in the daylight, Venus appeared saggier than Miller remembered, as if she had deflated in her sleep. Compared to Meg, taut from astronaut training, she seemed like another species, something lithe Meg would wear out on a spacewalk.

"Oh my God," Venus said. "Are you talking to people in outer space?"

Miller told Venus to put some clothes on, but Venus moved her nakedness in front of him, her naked self right in front of the camera. One of her breasts stopped in front of the camera and was centered on Meg's screen, a pink target, inset in the corner of the laptop, her nipple where Miller's face had just been.

"How far are you from Venus?" Venus said. "That's my name you know, 'Venus.'"

Meg stared at the screen. Another astronaut, one of the Russians, noticed Meg's screen and stopped what he was doing.

"Venus, your clothes," Miller said. He put his hands on her hips to move her out of the way.

"Oops!" Venus said, half-covering herself, and scurried toward the bedroom. On her way, she bent over to pick up her black bra and panties, presenting herself to everyone watching. Venus looked back at the screen from between her legs and waved, saying, "Bye-bye!" before disappearing into the bedroom.

"Meg," Miller said.

"Oh, Miller," Meg said, and hung up on him. From space.

Miller drove Venus back to her car in the Walmart lot. She'd wanted a tour of the base, asked if Miller could take her up in a plane. When Miller said that wasn't possible, she said she'd settle for pancakes. They stopped for drive-through instead, which

Miller paid for, and when they got to Venus's car, Venus made Miller dial her number into his phone and hit SEND.

"I don't mind long-distance relationships," she said, glancing up at the sky and winking.

"Good one," Miller said. He would need to erase the contact, maybe even get a new phone and number, but it didn't alter the Skype incident that morning.

Venus called Miller four times in his hour drive back to Cape Canaveral, once to tell him she missed him, once to tell him she'd left her panties at his house, once to tell him she'd left the panties on purpose and that she'd hidden them and he'd have to find them, and once to ask if Meg was really his wife and not his sister. The last three Miller let go to voicemail; when he listened to them later, his heart sank: Venus was crying during the last one. He'd done a number on two women today, a personal record by two.

At the shuttle headquarters, Miller tried to use his ID to get into Mission Control, but the guards told him his clearance had been revoked. No matter what he said, he couldn't get past them, and they strongly indicated that he should stop asking. His plan had been to ask MC to call the station so he could talk to Meg. He even pictured everyone leaving the room, all the techies and military personnel, giving them some privacy, as if NASA would leave a trillion dollars of equipment unattended so he could work out his marital issues. He was lucky he wasn't arrested, let alone cut out.

Two days later, Meg was supposed to Skype him again at 11 a.m. and Miller sat at his laptop from ten until just after noon, waiting. Nothing. Two days after that, nothing again. Meg wouldn't be back for another three months and Miller couldn't bear it. A week after Venus, Miller saw Meg on CNN, in the background of an interview with the mission commander, Meg holding a clipboard, floating in the air, taking readings from a panel of dials. It made Miller regret everything more, to see her working, not trying to wave, not tapping her nose, the special signal they'd invented.

By the end of Meg's first month in space, Miller spent all his time in their yard, just hoping Meg would be spying on him. Miller splayed himself out on the back lawn, lying there for hours at first, then entire days. He called in sick, then took official leave. By then, everyone knew what he'd done and nobody wanted him around, anyway. He lay spread-eagle in the tall, unkempt grass, on one side of him his laptop, just in case Meg decided to reach out, and on the other, some water and a package of saltines. On his chest he rested a sign, facing it toward the sky. It read, "MEG, I'M SORRY. COME HOME SOON."

# THE PLUM TREE

1

"Most plums are filled with worms," you tell my parents, the first thing you say to them, allergies making it look like you're weeping.

2

You in Denver, I stymie the trunk with copper nails, gather the strays, dry them on ledges, count the days till they're prunes.

3

You say plums remind you of our wedding, and when I ask how, you remember it was apricot compote filling our cake, you insisting apricots and plums are basically the same fruit.

4

The bleeding slowed, I fed you cobbler in bed, asked where we'd spend our next anniversary, you already asleep, sugar crusting your lips, your tongue dashing out for a taste.

5

A blackbird, plum in beak, lands on the porch, drops the gnarled fruit, flies off, and you bury its pit opposite the already-grown tree, explaining what a waste it would be for the gesture to go unrewarded.

6

We flew to Oakland, taxied to Saratoga, drank wine for three days, celebrating nine years, your tongue smelling of our back yard, fermenting in my mouth.

7

The June the boy plummeted from above, breaking his neck, a plum with one bite clasped in his hand, we were married ten years, long enough to know we'd never have kids of our own, grateful we'd never bear ourselves what we'd have to tell his parents.

8

From DC, you write how the cherry blossoms remind you of me, of us, but not enough to bring you home.

9

The hearing months away, you text from the bus, wonder if you'd made a mistake, if it was too late; hammer in hand, I let you drive farther away, far enough to be too late.

10

The stump chars with a sizzle, sweet syrup choking the wind, the pile of plums atop popping like corn in a kettle.

11

Our eleventh anniversary, the last, we fly to Spain, make love nine times in a week, eat dessert after every meal, burn then peel from the sun, both of us knowing we can make it if only we never have to go home.

12

Pliny the Elder, Roman historian, claimed that apricots were the first plums, found in Mesopotamia, the first civilization, purple emerging centuries later, your boasting emerging much more quickly.

13

The pit from the blackbird's plum sprouts but I stomp it down, one plum tree in any yard enough, too much.

# PLAGUES OF EGYPT

Plague of blood: Ex. 7:14–25

I found the reddened rags in the bottom of the garbage, hidden under coffee grounds, egg shells, and spoiled beef. I want to ask you about them but don't, figuring you didn't bury bloodied rags only to have me ask you about them later. I scan your body for cuts in the shower the next morning and find none, then wonder if your wounds are internal, if you're spitting it up, bleeding from the nose, something worse. We make love that night and I consider how the blood might not be yours, that you've tenderly tended to whomever that blood belonged.

Plague of frogs: Ex. 7:25–8:15

We find the dead frog in the bottom of the coffee can, three weeks after breaking the seal, explaining why our coffee has tasted putrid, why we've been getting sick, even why you'd gotten that wart on your finger. The coffee company doesn't believe us when we send a picture, accusing us of faking it so we can cash in, but then six more cases surface that week, frogs inside pudding and yogurt, one floating in a bottle of root beer. The next morning we don't have coffee, save frog coffee, but brew a pot, swearing it'd be our last.

Plague of lice or gnats: Ex. 8:16–19

The boys next door play baseball in their yard with their heads shaved. I watch them from my bathroom window, six boys born in seven years, two-thirds a team, their mother, the catcher, pregnant again, hoping for a girl, the father, on the mound and losing velocity, wanting that lefty reliever, all six so far righties, though with power to the opposite side. That night the father peeks over the fence, warns me they all have lice, even the mom, but she refuses to go bald, insisting the baby will be female if she can just keep her luscious hair.

Plague of flies or wild animals: Ex. 8:20–32

Oranges the size of grapefruits speck our front yard, ten years since we bothered picking, bothered picking up. The day you leave, I come home to find the rotting spheres stacked like cannonballs. Inside, you've already packed, called for a taxi, cover your ears when I try to talk. You say the stack is a gift to me, order out of chaos, beauty emerged from death. After I can't stop you from leaving me, I sit on the porch three days, eat as many oranges as I can, the gnats stuck to my fingers just as sweet, immersed in juice.

Plague of pestilence: Ex. 9:1–7

Our first date ended with us both getting mono, one of us the culprit passer, so we didn't see each other again for six weeks. When we returned to school, everyone made kissing noises as we passed, and the principal, school nurse, and health teacher called a meeting for our parents, warning us not to spread it to anyone else. After, you tried to kiss me, but your father pulled you away, told us there'd be no more of that, then I pulled you back closer, kissed you right in front of him, the gap in between already too long, agony.

Plague of boils: Ex. 9:8–12

She calls me the first time since she left, not to talk, not to say she's sorry, certainly not to reconcile, but to ask me to lance a boil. It's in the center of her back, out of arms' reach, a swollen Mars. Not only can't she sit back in a chair; its position against her spine means she feels it when she walks, each step a jolt. I arrive in the morning, lay her on her kitchen counter, press into it with my thumbs—the pustule breaks inside her, she screams, and I know she feels what I've felt.

Plague of hail: Ex. 9:13–35

We share an umbrella in a field of lupines, the air hot and thick, marveling at the shards streaking from the sky. The umbrella is small and we take the brunt of the blasts on our backs. The lupines don't fare well, the hail hard and fast enough to sever their stalks, thousands of them falling around us until the entire field is lost. We gather as many as our umbrella will hold, carry them three miles home, and fill our bathtub. We hold each other and inhale the smell, the air never so clean, our bodies piebald with welts.

Plague of locusts: Ex. 10:1–20

Forty years ago my wife took a painting class at the local college and after weeks of still lifes of fruit and vases and cones and spheres, she painted a giant locust, three feet tall and two feet wide, an overhead shot, bulging eyes at the top, melodious legs pointed south. Behind the locust she etched the word for locust in over two hundred languages, some I've still never heard of. For forty years, it's hung in our living room above the long couch, and to this day, I can't recall the word for "locust" in any language except ours.

Plague of darkness: Ex. 10:21–29

Last night I dreamed I couldn't open my eyes. I was driving down a road through the woods, my daughter in the backseat, and without warning, my eyelids sealed as if stitched. I swerved awkwardly, put the car in park, and got out, waving my hands in the air, hoping to flag someone down, proclaiming blindness. Our daughter, belted in her seat, was trapped, screaming. My eyes were walnuts then and I heard a deer cross the road behind me, its hooves clicking on the blacktop. I fell to my knees and felt for the yellow dashes, for the center.

Death of the firstborn: Ex. 11:1–12:36

I refuse to write this last part, my son asleep in the room next door, today his first day of school. On the way, he claimed that his blood hurt, that it was hard, that he wanted to stay home. I made him go but worried all day, looked up "hard blood" on the Internet, called my doctor, and arrived to pick him up an hour early. For dinner we ate chocolate ice cream and he described the book his teacher read after lunch, about a boy who only ate ketchup and turned into a French fry, a pretty unlikely story.

# BULLFIGHTING

The night after my husband's funeral, my son started talking to a man in his bedroom. At first I thought it was Shane, his dead father, his ghost, maybe a photo. When the conversations persisted, getting louder and more animated, I pressed my ear to the door. Hunter wasn't talking to his dad, but to a man named Lewis. They talked about kids at school, toys Hunter wanted me to buy him, foreign countries he wanted to visit. Lewis was from Spain, so they discussed Spain, which Hunter knew a lot about. They also talked about me.

"She said I won't be sad one day," Hunter told him.

"She's right," Lewis said.

Hunter's voice for Lewis was deep and gravelly, the voice of a friendly monster.

"I don't believe it," Hunter said.

"She loves you."

Hunter had to know I was outside the door. I heard him beat his fists into his pillow. I was about to go inside when I heard the Lewis' voice again.

"Calm down, Buddy. It's going to be OK."

And Hunter calmed down.

Hunter and Lewis talked to each other for two weeks before I was introduced. One afternoon I heard Hunter's window break and I rushed up to his room. Hunter had one shoe on, the other through the window. A cut the shape of half a heart bled from his forearm. As I cleaned and bandaged him in the bathroom, I established a door rule, that they were open, except for the bathroom, from now on.

"Lewis thinks that's a good idea, too."

"Who's Lewis?" I asked.

"My best friend."

"Did Lewis throw your shoe through your window?"

"No. He tried to stop me."

"Maybe you should listen to Lewis."

"Maybe," Hunter said, looking proud at his array of Band-Aids. "Can Lewis have one, too?"

The bedroom conversations with Lewis stopped with the door open, but things otherwise grew worse. Hunter and I occupied the same spaces without speaking. As soon as I'd leave a room, he and Lewis would talk about me. My mac and cheese was runny. Taking out the garbage sucked. I was putting on weight.

I tried spoiling him. We went to the park. We played laser tag. I downloaded apps onto my iPad. We went out to the pizza buffet five straight nights. All the toys and video games he told Lewis about, I bought. Hunter would play them for an hour, then get bored. Sometimes he'd never even open the package, a seventy-dollar game. If I returned it, he'd accuse me of stealing.

I called the school one morning to make an appointment with the counselor, what I should have done as soon as Shane died.

"He can help you, too," the secretary said, and I asked her what she meant.

"Which day sounds good?" she asked.

The night before the first session, I explained to Hunter where we'd be going after school on Wednesdays. Hunter said a kid named Jamie saw the counselor on Tuesdays. Jamie liked to stab himself with pencils, right in the arm, sometimes hitting a vein. It was to get out of tests. Hunter asked if he was like Jamie: crazy. I told him no.

"So don't make me go."

"You're going," I said.

"You should go. I'll sit in the hall with Lewis."

"Lewis can come inside, too."

"Whatever," Hunter said and went to the bathroom and shut the door. He and Lewis had a long talk. The word "hate" came before "mom" a lot. When he was done, he said he'd go to the appointment, but wouldn't talk and neither would Lewis. He went upstairs without saying good night.

I followed Hunter up an hour later and I cried in bed. I put my face in my pillow so Hunter couldn't hear, but then stopped trying to muffle myself. I slammed my head into the pillow, over and over. I wanted Hunter to come running. I wanted him to care.

When I heard footsteps, I felt embarrassed to need attention from an eleven-year-old. I tried lying still, fake-sleeping.

"Are you OK?"

It was Lewis' voice asking, not Hunter's.

I stuck with the fake-sleeping, hoping Hunter would go back to bed. Lewis asked again, "Are you OK?"

I ripped the covers off and turned around. I was ready to lay into Hunter, for what I don't know.

Hunter wasn't standing in front of me. It was a man, dressed in jeans and a denim button-down shirt, a Band-Aid on his left hand. He had dark, curly hair and a thick black mustache with eyebrows to match.

"I'm Lewis," he said. "It's good to meet face to face."

Dr. Hooke looked too young to be a school psychologist. He couldn't have been thirty and his shelves were filled with toys, My Little Ponies and Wolverines and three types of zombies. I whispered to Lewis that Dr. Hooke could have been an eighth-grader, posing as the shrink. We snickered

"Something funny?" Dr. Hooke asked.

"No, sir." I grabbed a handful of candy from the bowl on his desk.

Before the meeting, I'd filled out a battery of paperwork, relaying the complete mental and physical history of my family, of Shane's, and of me and Hunter. I'd had a great-aunt with schizophrenia, and my paternal grandfather had PTSD post-Korea. Shane had died when a piece of debris from a crane fell through the roof of his car as he drove underneath. He was otherwise slated to live to a hundred.

I focused on Shane's death. Hunter, for the first time, talked about it, too, saying he missed his dad, declaring it unfair this didn't happen to other kids.

"It does," Dr. Hooke said.

"None I know."

When Lewis came up, Hunter told Dr. Hooke that Lewis'd lost his dad, too, in the bullfighting ring, his dad gored a thousand times when all the bulls got loose at once. Lewis trained for five years then killed all the bulls with a katana. After, he stowed away on a boat to America, the Spanish government after him. He moved in with us the night of Shane's funeral.

"Is Lewis in the room now?" Dr. Hooke asked.

"No," Hunter said.

"Sweetie, tell the truth," I said. Lewis squeezed my hand.

"I'm not lying. Lewis went to the mall."

"Hunter!" I yelled.

"He's not here," Hunter insisted.

"Maybe one day Lewis will want to come and see me," Dr. Hooke said. "I'd love to meet him."

"He's protective of me," Lewis whispered, then nodded at Dr. Hooke, who was too full of himself to nod back.

After dinner, I suggested we play a board game, something I bought that Hunter hadn't opened. We started to read over rules to Aggravation, but Hunter got bored and watched TV. He went to bed early. I started a game of Aggravation, playing for all six players, until all of their marbles reached their bases. When I went upstairs, I saw Hunter's door closed and went to open it—the policy still in effect—but heard Lewis and Hunter talking about Dr. Hooke. I knocked and said good night and got one back from both of them.

I couldn't have been out long when Lewis woke me. He was sitting on the edge of my bed.

"It looked like fun," he said.

"Is that what you talked about?"

"Hunter's warming up to you. He wants you to be friends, like him and his dad."

"We're not friends?"

Lewis patted my thigh through the covers.

"I'm sorry about your dad. The bulls," I said.

"It's my country's embarrassment, what they do to those creatures."

"But you killed them all."

"And that is my embarrassment."

Lewis' face was covered in stubble, surrounding his mustache. In the dark, I couldn't tell the color of his eyes.

"Lie back," Lewis said and got up to shut the door.

When Hunter came downstairs the next morning, I had bacon and eggs and sausages on the table, along with toast, juice, milk, and his vitamins. His clothes for school were laid out on his chair and his book bag waited by the door, a signed permission slip for a field trip inside.

"What's this?" he said.

"A solid breakfast. You have gym today. We meet with Dr. Sharpe, too."

Hunter had grown used to pouring cereal and milk into a bowl, often the bowl from the morning before, specks of cereal stuck to the sides.

Hunter punctured his yolks. Yellow oozed like chaos.

"Is everything all right, Mom?"

"Perfect."

Hunter wolfed down everything and brushed his teeth. We got out the door on time, a first. On the way, I told Hunter Lewis would be staying with us on a permanent basis. He would sleep in my room—I had the bigger bed—and Lewis was someone he needed to listen to.

"Like Dad?"

"Not like Dad," I said. "Exactly like Dad."

The next couple of weeks flew. We kept up the morning routine. Hunter performed better at school. At night, we spoke. We weren't old biddies at the parlor, but he acknowledged my presence. Even Dr. Hooke noticed a difference.

"Hunter says you're now getting out of bed in the morning," he said.

"You know, the most important meal of the day."

Lewis still resisted Dr. Hooke, wondering if maybe he was a Spanish agent, a mole, waiting for Lewis to reveal himself. I doubted Dr. Hooke capable of such stealth, but I didn't think we'd need his services much longer, anyway.

Lewis and I got to spend the days together. The settlement from the construction company meant I didn't have to run out and get a job. Lewis said when he escaped, he'd grabbed some crown jewels. He'd never have to work again.

Maybe it was too soon, but I thought about Lewis, his immigration problems, about how much I'd grown to need him. Marriage would fix a lot of those problems. Then I'd feel better about revealing our relationship to Hunter. He'd get a dad. I'd get what I'd been getting. I waited for the right moment to bring it up, but suspected that Lewis was thinking exactly what I was thinking.

Then one day, Lewis and I were in bed, so wrapped up in ourselves that we lost track of the time. I looked up at one point to see Hunter, wearing his backpack, staring down at us horror.

"What are you doing, Mommy?" he asked. I was naked, sweating, my legs splayed.

"Yoga," I said. Lewis was in the bathroom. I pulled a sheet up to my neck.

"Why didn't you pick me up?"

"How'd you get home?"

"I walked," Hunter said. "It's raining."

"I'm so sorry," I said. "Lewis and I feel terrible."

"Don't blame Lewis," Hunter said.

"It's both our faults."

"No, it's not. Lewis doesn't even like you."

I slapped Hunter across the face. He was wet and cold. As if I couldn't have felt worse. I tried to grab him, but he ran into his room, slamming his door.

Lewis came out of the bathroom.

"What happened?" he asked, and I explained.

Lewis went inside Hunter's room. I heard the two of them talking, then Hunter screaming, but I let Lewis handle it. Like Hunter said, Lewis was his friend, not mine.

Downstairs, I found several messages on my phone from the school, asking when I was coming to pick Hunter up. The last wanted me to verify a story about Hunter remembering he was supposed to walk to a friend's and he'd forgotten. Last was a call from Dr. Hooke, saying we'd missed our appointment.

I made dinner, just a frozen pizza, but sprinkled extra cheese on top, something Shane used to do. When it was done, I ate a third of it, then went to get Lewis and Hunter. Hunter would have been calmed down by then, and maybe, if I was lucky, he'd talk to me.

Halfway up the stairs, I heard a loud crash, then Hunter yell, "No!" When I went I went inside Hunter's room, he was alone. The window, which I'd just had fixed, was broken again, this time the entire pane shattered.

"What happened? Where's Lewis?"

"He's gone," Hunter said. "He said he couldn't be my friend anymore."

"Don't lie to me. Where is he?"

Hunter looked out the window.

I ran down the stairs, ignoring the glass, the cuts on Hunter's hands. Hunter chased me, asking where I was going. I told him I was going after Lewis. I promised to bring him back.

"You can't," Hunter said.

"Why not?"

"Because he's dead."

I grabbed Hunter by his head. "What do you mean, he's dead?"

"The Spaniards came," he said.

"The Spaniards?"

"Lewis wouldn't be taken alive. He yelled that, 'You'll never take me alive!' Then he bit down on a cyanide capsule in his tooth. White foam dripped from his gums and his eyes rolled into the back of his head. The spies threw his body in a trunk and drove off right before you came in my room."

I didn't want to believe what Hunter was saying. Lewis couldn't be dead.

I pulled Hunter close to me. I looked out the front door for the Spaniards. I felt alone. Then I felt terrified. How had they tracked Lewis to our house? And now that he was dead, would they come for Hunter and me next?

# NIGHT OF THE SCALLOP

The day we discovered Burla's allergy to shellfish was the same day we found the portal to another dimension between our mattress and box springs. Two swollen eyelids, an engorged pair of lips, and a closed trachea will get you to the hospital, but six lost dust ruffles will render an even quicker call to the exorcist. Burla, a quadruple dose of antihistamine later, breathed regularly by midnight, but the exorcist made us wait out the night.

"Negative zone," he said the next afternoon. "Classic case."

I asked if Burla's newfound allergy was related, since Burla was forty-three and hadn't had this reaction before. Before the exorcist could pose much of a theory, Burla interrupted, revealing to this stranger that the deadly scallops may have been the first shellfish she'd ever eaten. *Hold on*, I thought. *How's it possible to reach forty-three without ever trying shellfish?* The exorcist packed his gear and handed us a bill, reminding us not to waste any more money on dust ruffles.

For weeks, Burla shuffled around the bed like she was afraid of it, sleeping in the middle, careful to put her hair up and the comforter down. With Burla in the center, I was forced to the couch. Earlier in our relationship, we'd shared a bed, but kept to opposite sides, me too restless, Burla needing time to think our predicament over. Once we found out about the negative zone that lurked below, my tossing and kicking would've freaked her out. The one time, post-exorcist, we gave sleeping together a go, the night after the night of the scallops, Burla woke from sleep terrors, dreaming of emptiness, of getting stuck in a dark tunnel, the tunnel that was flooding, Burla unable able to escape. It was her brain's projection of the negative zone, my A in Psych 101 was screaming, no real basis of comparison available to her. Since the inside of the couch hid nothing but chip crumbs, loose change, and a twin sleeper, I set up camp.

The shitty thing about the whole situation was that Burla ate the scallops—the *scallop*—on our wedding night, the one night, if any, you're supposed to share a bed with your wife. We'd had a sweet ceremony, and even though the reception was small, love was in the air. But who would ever guess Burla would turn lavender the exact moment this interdimensional portal opened in our bed? I mean really, forty-three and no crab legs? No lobster? Not a single shrimp? How is that even possible? Didn't any other guy ever take her out to dinner?

Before he died, my dad had the talk with me about my wedding night, what I should expect, and how I should act. He'd never figured I'd be thirty-eight when it came, but he also never filled me in on the intricacies, the nuances. Tonight, as I lie alone on the twin sleeper for the umpteenth night, I worry that Burla will fall into the negative zone, that I'll wake to find her gone, leaving me a newlywed widower. Even worse, I think about Dad's advice, to respect my wife, that your first night together sets the tone for your entire marriage. Every time I hear these words in my head, I want to go into the bedroom, dump Burla from the mattress, dive into that other dimension, and find my dead father. Then I want to crack him in the jaw, tell him he had no idea. Not a fucking clue.

# OPAL FOREVER

Griffin spent fourteen years loving a woman named Opal, living with her, planning to die with her. He bought her a house and they filled it with appliances, photos, furniture, and art. They took vacations, overseas to places like Honduras and Iceland, stateside to Provincetown, Sedona, and Eureka Springs. Their families spent holidays together, Christmas every year, alternating Thanksgivings and Easters, and they loved pets, fish and turtles and parakeets, mostly a golden retriever named Sunbeam they mourned when she ran away. They had no children, but spoiled their nieces, nephews, and friends' kids as much as they could afford. On their tenth anniversary, Opal got a heart tattoo with a *G* and an *O* inside on her inside right ankle, while Griffin got an oblong heart that said *Opal Forever* on his left forearm, candy-apple red with gothic black letters, stretching from elbow to wrist, the point of the heart curling into a vine on the back of his hand. Opal joked that if they ever broke up, she'd have a heart with the word *GO* inside, but Griffin would have to find another woman named Opal. Griffin replied, "You'd take me for an arm and a leg, so I guess we know which arm you can have."

Three years after the tattoos, Opal left Griffin for another teacher at her elementary school, a younger, red-haired woman named Jeannette who played the harp and wore flowing, tie-dyed skirts. For a year, living in their house while Opal lived in Jeannette's apartment, Griffin worked to get Opal back, to convince her the other woman was a phase, that he could be a better man, whatever Opal wanted him to be. After that year, Opal and Jeannette married, adopted twin boys from Laos, and bought a golden retriever puppy, naming it Moonbeam. Griffin knew he was through.

Griffin sold Opal and Jeannette the house, and aside from his clothes and the set of dishes from his godmother, he left everything. Settled in an apartment, in a student complex near the college, he decided to find someone who wouldn't get tired of him. Griffin had one requirement for this new woman: she had to be named Opal, too.

Griffin's remaining friends hoped his obsession had nothing to do with the OPAL FOREVER tattoo on his arm. To this, Griffin always replied, "It has everything to do with the tattoo on my arm." He'd made a choice, years earlier, to love an Opal forever, and if it took him forever, he was going to do it.

One couple, the Nevelsons, bought him a watch for his birthday, the face an inset opal. Griffin was not amused, hiding the watch in his bathroom under the towels. His best friend, Parker, took him to a strip club where a dancer named Opal Rain feature-danced. Griffin bought a lap dance from this Opal, and behind a beaded curtain, he rolled up his sleeve, showed her dancer his tattoo, and proposed. He said, "I will love you for the rest of my life." Minutes later, he and Parker were removed from the club at Opal Rain's behest.

"Too bad Opal's name wasn't Brittany," said Parker, married with four kids. "Most clubs I go to have three or four of those."

Knowing that women named Opal in his city were scarce, Griffin broadened his search. He signed up for several dating websites, ranging from the most benign, to meat markets, to sites where he didn't fit the profile, not leaving anything to chance. Most sites rejected him. Those that didn't required that he localize his search to a specific geographic region, but Griffin was willing to long-distance online-date anyone, as long as her name was Opal. He received an impressive number of replies, some from Opals looking just for sex, some from Opals not specifically women, and some from Opals who became possibilities—until Griffin e-mailed them a picture of his OPAL FOREVER tattoo, proposed, and told them he would love them for the rest of his life.

By the end of the first day, Griffin had turned off every person named Opal in the U.S., Puerto Rico, the Virgin Islands, and Guam, yet he didn't give up hope. It might take longer than a day, and he hadn't even tried Canada. His passport was in his glove box, ready to go.

When the Internet Opals stopped responding, Griffin fretted over never finding anyone. He sulked, resigning himself to dying alone, his tattoo a lie.

"You could have it altered, even removed," Parker suggested.

Griffin called this bad karma, to mangle something so beautiful.

To pass his days, he let Parker practically move in. They ate carry-out, played video games, watched sporting events neither of them cared about, and at Parker's request, drank the absinthe he'd bought online from the Czech Republic. Whenever Parker had to go home—his wife, Jade, was losing patience—Griffin would show up at their house, sit in their family room, and play with their kids. Their oldest two, Rebecca and Amanda, remembered him and Opal, the happy couple who took them places and bought them gifts. The third child, Sean, asked Griffin if he was the crazy man in love with Oprah, then kicked Griffin in the balls for touching his Legos.

While at Parker's house one day, Griffin received a reply on his phone from a dating site, a local one, from a woman named Opal who wanted to meet right away. She claimed to be freshly divorced yet ready for a commitment. Griffin, restraining himself, didn't send the tattoo photo or a proposal, and agreed to meet. He tracked down Parker, who was hiding in his basement, and told him he had a lead. Parker warned him not to get too excited, even offered to go with, but Griffin drove to the diner alone, where the new Opal had set up the rendezvous. He sat at the counter, holding off on ordering, waiting for his new love.

While waiting, Griffin ignored five calls and four texts from Parker, likely requests for pie, the diner's specialty. When this Opal was an hour late, Griffin ordered a piece of custard. Just as he finished, Parker came through the door with his baby, Parker, Jr., in tow and told Griffin it was a goof: The Opal that Griffin was meeting was him, an excuse for them to get out of the house. Griffin would have punched Parker in the mouth if the latter hadn't been carrying a three-month-old baby. Parker begged Griffin to stay for pie, his treat, and Griffin handed Parker his bill.

Griffin remained furious at Parker for weeks, but he also felt grateful. He had been stupid. The chances of a woman named Opal being the one, let alone finding him, were astronomical. After all, it'd already happened once. He was starting to see just how crazy living at the mercy of a tattoo had made him act. He had other tats that didn't carry any meaning, namely the Black Flag bars on his other wrist—he hadn't listened to them in years and now thought Henry Rollins was a putz. The barbed wire that surrounded his left thigh didn't have purpose—Who was he trying to keep out of his leg?—and neither did the spiderweb spun over his right elbow. When he was nineteen, being badass was his M.O., and when he was thirty-three, sacrificing a forearm for Opal seemed romantic. He would always have the tattoo, and if he ever met someone else, she probably wouldn't like it much. But if she was who Griffin imagined, it wouldn't matter. It was just a fucking tattoo.

Griffin refocused. Despite having money—he did website consulting for high-end professionals—he'd been living like a college student, pizza boxes stacked on his kitchen floor, laundry nights in a communal basement. He bought a small Victorian in the older section of town, planted tomatoes, squash, and sugar peas out back, and started running around his neighborhood, a mile a day, then two, training for a Labor Day 5K. He adopted a shelter mutt he named Tattoo and brought him along on his runs. He forgave Parker, whose elaborate apologies—he claimed he'd hired a skywriter, which Griffin never saw—became more annoying than the ruse at the diner. Griffin had also been ignoring the alerts from the dating sites and took down his profiles. The last site he went to cancel, the most local, had only one reply in its in box, two months old: It was from Opal, the genuine and original. She had wanted to meet.

Misgivings aside, Griffin answered Opal's request, sure of himself and glad he'd received it when he did. It had been sent at a time when he was more vulnerable, just a few days after the Parker fallout. Griffin suspected that his friend, wanting to get back in good graces, had asked Opal to send it. Griffin didn't care. He felt good, looked good, and he knew he would run into Opal sooner or later, anyway, the town just not that big. He agreed to meet, and after three days without a reply, Opal wrote and arranged coffee at their once-favorite cafe, Febrewary, for the next morning.

Griffin arrived early and secured a table on the sidewalk. He made sure to bring a newspaper, not wanting to be caught staring down the street. When Opal arrived and sat down, Griffin told her she looked well and asked about Jeannette and the twins. They were fine, Opal assured, adding something about how different they were despite being identical. Griffin told Opal about his house, Tattoo, and some new clients, including his father's security company, plus the lawyer on the infamous billboards with the eye patch, a local celebrity.

"Does he really only have one eye?" Opal said. Griffin said he hadn't inquired.

They split four slices of biscotti draped in dark chocolate, then just like that, Opal said she had to leave. Griffin, confused about this whole scenario, asked outright: "Why are we here?" Opal said it was nice to catch up, that maybe they could be friends, but Griffin pressed her: "Why not call?" Opal claimed she was worried about him. Griffin asked if Parker had put her up to this, and Opal said no, though Parker had confronted her often right after the breakup, begging her to change her mind, even showing up at her and Jeannette's wedding, ready to pound on the choir loft glass. She hadn't heard from him since they'd adopted the twins.

"Then why the dating site?"

Opal picked up her empty coffee cup and tried to drink, then waved at the barista for more, frustrated he didn't see her. She cursed, which Griffin had never heard before.

Griffin suddenly knew the truth. "You were there looking to meet someone else, weren't you?"

Opal denied this charge and threatened to leave. But she didn't leave. She accused Griffin of stalking her, then calmed herself and began to cry. Things with Jeannette weren't perfect, she said. Things between her and Griffin hadn't been perfect, either, but she admitted to giving it all up too quickly. "We had a commitment," Opal said, looking down at the OPAL FOREVER heart on Griffin's arm.

"It's just a tattoo," Griffin said. "It's not a contract."

Opal insisted that tattoos meant something, and when Griffin tried to argue, pointing at his web, Opal took off the shoe and sock from her right foot, showing him what she'd done: The G and O inside her heart tattoo now said, GRIFFIN + OPAL. From the redness and swelling, Griffin knew the work was recent, as recently as within the last twenty-four hours.

Griffin told Opal to keep her sock and shoe off unless she wanted an infection, then stood up and kissed Opal on her forehead. Into her ear, he whispered, "I will love you for the rest of my life." He walked away despite her calling out, and broke into a run, his house just a few miles away.

# THIN AIR

The magician has lost his hat and I can't bear to tell him he's losing me, too.

Boise, Butte, Missoula, Fargo, the Twin Cities for a double bill. I'd been disappearing since the Coast, somewhere between Sacramento and Seattle, vanished into the Persian Vault of Mystery, conjured away by the wave of his wand, sawed in half more times than I can count. Mathematicians say that no matter how many times you cut something in half, it will never go completely away, that you can halve it through infinity, the pieces becoming more and more microscopic. I may not be fading the same way, but I wonder what the math geniuses would say about me, what theories they would exact.

Hatless, the magician has not only lost half his tricks, but something more ephemeral. Hat on, the magician had performed with confidence, as much dancer as showman, his grace as vibrant as any of the colored hankies up his sleeve, any flash of fire from his 43, no blood, no pain, not even the loss of balance. Despite some initial worry, I ignored it, not wanting to add to the trauma already tainting the tour—I even fooled myself to thinking I was born that way. My sleight of hand failed when the toe's twin vanished as well. Something was amiss. Perhaps a miscarried trick I couldn't recall (among so many of late), an accident while unloading the truck. Or, maybe, this was some last-ditch enchantment on the part of the magician, a paltry attempt to woo. When I woke without the nape of my neck, my beating heart exposed, I knew this trick was beyond the magician's power, with hat or without. Though had I long hoped for him to tap into such an expanse, he was clearly incapable of any such feat. Near the end, I began to wonder if misfortune was somehow in control, his despair making possible a magic he'd never realized on his own.

While the magician plods on, town to town, stage to stage, miscue to miscue, I remain at his side, enduring my role until my shortcomings become obvious. I can move from fishnet to black hose, dispose of plunging necklines, wear gloves longer than my arms. Sooner or later, something more obvious than my heart will be exposed, and no piece of clothing, no rhinestone necklace, no feather accouterment, will be able to hide it. One day I'll vanish entirely, into, as he says, thin air. This is how I'll tell him, when he sees for himself, when it's too late to bring me back, no matter how hard he'll try. Until then, the parts of me that haven't faded will wave with flamboyant charm, scissor into dramatic poses, flash smiles for the ages, waiting to serve as the grand finale.

# MARROW

In the Price Cutter parking lot, a woman is masturbating in her Oldsmobile. She's in the driver's seat, tilted back forty-five degrees, and it looks like she's trying to squeeze her eyes out of the back of her head. It's noon. I walk inside the store, grab lighter fluid, and as I pay, I say to the checkout kid and the bagger, "By the way, there's a woman jacking it out there in her car." The bagger kid stares at me—he doesn't get it—but the checkout guy, he shoves my receipt in my hand and yells, "Break!" to the manager, and turns off his aisle light before sprinting outside ahead of me. Three other customers wait behind me in line.

Outside, the cashier guy is looking around two rows over. When he sees me outside, he runs up and grabs my bag and says, "Let me get that for you." When we reach my car, the woman is still at it. I linger. Her knees are at face level and I can see her right arm moving like she's trying to light a fire with sticks. I take the bag from the kid, who stares at the woman as I drive off, his hand still extended.

At the park, my brother Geoff is watching my sons. He's been staying with me since he got laid off and my wife left, unrelated events that happened the same week. My boys are five and three, and when I return from the store, they're both climbing the plastic rock wall; the sign next to the wall says, "12 and Over." Thirty yards from them, I have to scream because the little one is at the top, standing like King Kong swatting biplanes. Then he falls—right into Geoff's arms, as if that had been the plan.

"Little guy's a bug," Geoff says.

We find an open grill and I light the coals. The boys eat chips and drink grape pop and tell me Uncle Geoff wants to buy us matching tattoos. Geoff calls them liars, but Geoff is more tattoo than man so I believe them. I tell Geoff there was a hiring sign in the Price Cutter window and he admits the four of us getting tats—maybe pirate skulls or bear claws ripping out from inside us—would be "transcendent." The boys chase geese down at the pond and for some reason I tell Geoff about the woman in the Olds. Before I finish, he's jogging to my car, saying he'll bring some brats, maybe steaks. We already have steaks. Fifteen minutes later, Geoff pulls up with a package of hot dogs and the woman from the lot I saw masturbating.

"Susanna, this is my brother, Carl," Geoff says.

"I know Carl," Susanna says. "He was parked next to me at the store."

Susanna holds her hand out for me to shake. I hesitate to oblige.

Susanna eats steak, plays Ghost in the Graveyard, then comes home with us that night. Before Geoff asks, I forbid her from moving in. The next week, every night around two a.m., she and Geoff play-act a routine where they talk, in fake-quiet voices, about her having to go, then Geoff knocks on my door, asks to use my car to drive Susanna home. Susanna's home is her car, a car that is still parked at the Price Cutter. I tell him not to bother, that she can stay over. Geoff thanks me as if I've given him my marrow, folding his hands together and bowing like a monk. They scurry down to the basement, where they screw for an hour or two, then again a couple of hours later. By the second week, Geoff starts forgetting to knock on my door, apologizing in the morning, claiming they fell asleep watching a movie, though I still hear them having sex, which I assume they're awake for. It isn't until their romps wake the boys one morning, at six a.m., that I explain to Geoff about vents, how sound travels, what pillows are for. Geoff acts embarrassed, but he winks at me, tells me she can't control herself.

"Yeah," I say. "I got that."


Courtney caught me masturbating once not long before she left. I was in my office, my back to the door, headphones on, closed to the world. On my screen was a menagerie of browser windows, two rows of three, each playing a different video. My pants were bunched up around my ankles and I was squeezing the mouse like I was crushing it into a diamond. I was almost where I needed to be when Courtney tapped me on the shoulder. She was in front of me, her skin like the whites of her eyes. I didn't know if I should finish or ask Courtney to help, but Courtney went with option C, making me stop. She knelt in front of me and pulled up my pants, then yanked the power strip out of the wall. Then she had me restart the computer and delete my history, bookmarks, and over a thousand files I'd downloaded. She made me promise I wouldn't do anything like that again. I promised, and for months, I didn't. Then she left. I assumed it didn't matter after that.

With Susanna in the house, I've stopped masturbating again. Between the boys and Geoff and the vents, I hardly found the opportunity before. Now, I picture Susanna catching me. I'm in my office, nastiness on my screen, she comes in without me noticing. She waits for me to climax, hands me a tissue, and says, "Now we're even."

The boys start to call Susanna "Aunt Suzie." The first few times, I don't say anything because she's acting the part. She makes their lunches—in the middle of the night, between romps, I guess—and she picks them up from school even thought that's supposed to be Geoff's job. One night, while she and Geoff run for cigarettes, I tell the boys they should call her Susanna. They ask why and I say that she's not married to Uncle Geoff.

"Uncle Geoff told us to," the big one says.

"Uncle Geoff says a lot of things."

"But she's so nice. She taught me how to tie my shoes," the little one says, getting down on one knee to show me.

"I should have done that," I say.

"She's really pretty," the big one says. "She smells like raspberry jelly."

I explain how Uncle Geoff has a lot of girlfriends and that Aunt Suzie might not stay around much, that she could leave at any time.

"Like Mommy left?" the little one says. The tears start to well.

"Call her Aunt Suzie," I say. "She is pretty."

One evening, I have to work late one night. When I get home, nobody is around except for someone in the shower. I wait to see who it is—my kids don't take showers—and Susanna emerges, one towel around her head and one around her body. She says Geoff took the kids to a demolition derby a couple of towns over. They took a bus.

"Geoff's friend Tin Can drives a car," she says. "Geoff thinks Tin Can can get the boys a ride."

I should assume Susanna doesn't mean for an actual derby, to get smashed up, but ask anyway.

"Geoff's not stupid," she says. "They're just little kids."

I sit down in the front room because there's no dinner to make or homework to do. Susanna joins me, drying her hair on the couch opposite. She's a master contortionist the way she keeps the body towel in place while so vigorously rubbing her head with the other. Her body, the important parts, stays covered, but I still see tattoos I didn't know she had. Under her left arm, a topless mermaid sits on a rock holding a trident.

"So," she says. "Why'd your wife leave?"

Nobody has ever asked me that before, I realize, not even the kids. When Geoff wanted to move in, he didn't ask about Courtney, either, because Courtney had put up with zero of his shit. If she came back, he'd vacate the premises that instant.

Susanna waits for an answer, her hair sticking up and out from the static, the Bride of Frankenstein. I recall the incident in my office with the porn, but I'd been hoping it would be more complicated than that.

"Beats me," I say.

"Whatever it was, it was her problem," Susanna says. "Who could ever walk away from those precious little boys? Not to mention you."

I want to agree with the former, but then the Geoff comes in the door, a boy on each shoulder. All three of them are wearing black demolition derby shirts over their other shirts and have nacho cheese stains on their faces. Susanna gets up and disappears downstairs, but not before I see more tattoos, a revolver under each butt cheek, the smoking barrels pointed inward, between her legs.

"Guess who got to ride in a real demolition derby car?" the big one says. He has a fat lip and a Band-Aid over his left eye.

"It's not what you think," Geoff says. "He just fell off the bleachers."

Courtney calls on my birthday, her first contact in two months. We're about to sing and cut a cake Susanna made when Geoff spies my ringing phone and answers. He pretends he's me and that I'm having sex, panting in between responses to Courtney's questions, slapping his bare leg, breathing hard. Susanna picks up on it and starts moaning, yelling my name, "Oh, Carl, yeah! Harder, Carl! You fill me so good, Carl!" The boys are in the TV room wearing party hats and awaiting chocolate. I wait for Courtney to hang up, but Geoff says, "Yeah, it's me. How did you know?" and hands me the phone, after faking release, moaning, his eyes crossing.

"Geoff's there," Courtney says. "How nice."

She wants to talk to the kids; there's no way she remembers it's my birthday. I call them in and the looks on their faces tell all, smiles wrapping three times around their heads. As always, when one of the boys uses the magic words, *When are you coming home?* the next thing I hear is "She hung up" and I get handed my phone. Their eyes on the candles and the frosted mass, they don't cry.

"She thinks you were getting laid," Geoff whispers during "Happy Birthday," unable to suppress a belly laugh.

Geoff sleeps in one Saturday, a twelve-pack's worth of cans scattered on the kitchen counter. I find Susanna by the coffee maker when I wake, pouring me a cup. She asks if we have any waffles and when I say no, we never have any waffles, she says it's too bad because she and Geoff love waffles and I should think about keeping waffles in the freezer. I tell her there's a waffle iron somewhere in the basement, a wedding present I never opened, and she acknowledges this, says it's on a shelf right above their bed, but she never made the connection between that and having waffles. She'll sneak down and get the iron as soon as she's done with her coffee. She leans back in her chair, her knees out like butterfly wings, balancing her mug on her abdomen. Her shirt rises and I can see her tan stomach. I tell her we don't have the ingredients for waffles and offer to run to the store. She asks if I could check on her car, make sure it hasn't been towed.

"What if it has?" I ask.

"I'm out a car. And a house."

"Good thing Geoff likes you so much," I say.

"Good thing," she says and closes her legs.

"Anything besides the pancake batter?" I ask.

"We want waffles," she says, "not pancakes."

"It's the same batter for both," I say, then realize she's kidding.

"The kids are out of cereal," she says.

I get dressed and on my way out the door Susanna stops me. "That was meant for you, you know."

"Excuse me?" I say.

"I ended up here, anyway, which is weird, but that act in the parking lot, it was for you."

"You could have just introduced yourself."

"It worked," she says.

"Yeah—on Geoff."

"Exactly," she says. "That's why Geoff is Geoff and you're Carl. He knew what to do and here I am."

Susanna opens my coat and puts her arms around my waist.

"You know Geoff wasn't laid off," she says. "He quit the mill when he heard Courtney left."

I don't know what to say to this, or when Susanna stretches up on her toes to kiss me. I kiss her back, putting a hand on her shoulder and the other behind her head. I don't know if it's just on my brain, but her mouth tastes like raspberry jelly. I stop myself at that moment.

"Get out," I say. She tries to kiss me again, and again I start to kiss her back before making her stop. "Get out."

"Come on, Carl," she says, placing her fingers on the top button of my shirt, trying to work it through the hole.

I pull away from her and my button is ripped from my shirt, the pearly waste between her fingers. I explain to Susanna how serious I am, how I want her gone by the time I get back from the store. She tries to kiss me one more time and I call her a whore and push her away.

"That's better, Carl," she says. "That's what I'm talking about."

At the store I don't buy waffle mix or pancake mix or anything for Susanna or for Geoff, then wonder why I came. I grab bread and milk and apples and bananas and turn the corner to the cereal aisle when I realize I've left the boys at home, asleep in their room, perhaps no adults around if they wake up. Susanna has maybe left—I made myself clear—and Geoff lies blackout drunk two floors below. If they wake up and can't find anyone, anything could happen.

I leave the cart in front of the store by the checkout. One cashier is the kid I had the day I saw Susanna in the lot. He yells, "Is she out there again?" but I don't answer.

The whole ride home takes four minutes and I dread the worst, the older one run over by a car in the street, the little one floating facedown in the bathtub. I roll through a stop sign then drive through the next three. When I pull up, Geoff is sitting on the front stairs, drinking coffee and smoking. He tells me Susanna woke him, told him to see if the boys woke up, to watch them because I had to run out and she had to run out, too. Geoff asks if I was at the store and if I bought any waffles. I tell him no. Inside, Derek and David are still asleep, unaware I was gone. Geoff asks me where I think Susanna went and I tell him she went to check on her car. Geoff doesn't ask about how she got there or why we didn't go together, but instead says that we should all do something today, go to a movie, throw the Frisbee around in the yard, maybe go back to the park and do some grilling.

"That's where we met Susanna," he says.

"Sort of," I say.

"Yeah," he says.

Geoff takes a last drag on his cigarette and flicks the butt into the street where it comes to rest in a pothole puddle. It's not the only butt in the pool. Geoff tells me he's going back to bed, that I should wake him when I make a plan. At that moment, I know Geoff knows Susanna's gone for good, but he's OK with it, because we both know that she was never really there for him, anyway.

# HOME

This is what's transpired the past seven weeks: My son Max started seeing Brittany Schoenmeier, a cute girl he's known since kindergarten, dating for two weeks before cheating on her with Avery Constantini, another cute girl he's known all his life, making Brittany break up with him, but not hate him, because a week later, Brittany got back with my idiot son, not knowing he'd started dating Avery, whom Brittany has of course known all her life, too, leading to Max dating both girls for about a week, a glorious week for Max, I'm sure, until three hours apart last Saturday, Max found out both girls were pregnant with his child, leading Max into my study one night—admittedly, the kid looked like hell—to tell me he'd fathered not one, but two unplanned babies, Max seventeen, a B-minus student when he tried, never even having a paper route let alone a life plan, explaining to me how "the girls," Brittany and Avery, both wanted to keep his baby, both loving him so much, they were willing to not only love him, but all live together, under one roof, to form what Max called a "21$^{st}$-century family," the roof in this plan meaning my roof, as me and his mother were the only involved parties with a roof we could call our own, let alone any kind of money and—Max researched it—insurance to cover this whole mess, my plan good for everything for both girls if Max married one, got divorced, then married the other, as long as DNA amnis proved his paternity, which they did, resulting in me and my wife Jill in one room and Max, his ex-wife Avery, and his second wife Brittany sleeping down the hall, each girl four-and-a-half months pregnant, Max working at a pizzeria twenty hours a week with two months to go until graduation.

Jill's thrilled. She loves having the girls around—she loves the idea of two little babies running around, too. This is our blessing, she claims, for us to only have one child but two daughters-in-law, girls she oversaw in the lunch room, pointed out in school pictures, would run into at the mall, lovely and polite girls who already treat her like their mom; Avery's mom died ten years ago and Brittany's mom's a Bible-thumper who, along with her husband, has disowned Brittany, a promise I'm betting will stick. Jill's own mom has Alzheimer's, and her father goes blank whenever Jill explains Max's predicament, too depressed about his wife or perhaps because he doesn't believe her. My parents are both dead, but I have one brother, Matt, and his attitude is typical Matt: Max is the luckiest bastard on Earth, two nubile cuties camped in his bedroom, carrying his children, loving him, and the best part, Matt says, "Loving each other, too." I know what Matt's insinuating and I stop him before he gets going. Brittany and Avery are both underage, both call me "Dad," and neither of them is shy about crawling around the house in their underpants. Matt calms down, and in exchange, I don't throttle him.

There's only one person I can talk to about this situation: Avery's dad. I've known Jesse, like our kids, since kindergarten, and even though we weren't friends, in the twenty years since high school, we've reached the point of nodding if we pass each other on the street. Jesse hasn't been right since his wife died, never got anything like a career going. He and Avery shared a studio apartment, she on the couch bed and he in the easy chair down the hallway, him respecting her need to be a young woman. Jesse doesn't like any of this, either, and is embarrassed as shit. As often as he can, he visits Avery and Max (and, I guess, Brittany), drinks a couple of beers with me in the garage, and wants more than anything for us to invite him to live with us, eyeing the room across from the kids'. I counter this with comments like, "It must be nice to have some privacy, now that Avery's gone." Eventually, he'll offer help for when the babies come, buying the formula and diapers, maybe even one of those twin strollers, since my end is covered and Brittany's self-righteous parents won't contribute shit. I like Jesse and am glad we see eye to eye, but there's no way he's moving in. Jill jokes she could have two men if Max can have two women, a joke I find funnier every time she tells it.

Because God is hilarious, both girls go into labor the same day. It makes sense, I think, because Max admitted to impregnating both girls the same night, and also because—and this is my theory—the girls were cohabitating, in the same room, in the same bed, and their pregnancy cycles aligned—if it works that way for menstruation, why not?

The waiting room at the hospital proves as stressful as anyone would guess. Jesse excuses himself every half-hour and comes back drunker each time. Jill calls everyone she knows and sets Twitter update records. Max, whose life is about to become a lot less fantasy based, stares blankly at the Pepsi machine in front of him. Me, who half wants to be Jesse-drunk, half wants to be Jill-happy, tries to imagine how I'll handle it if something goes wrong, both girls so young, so tiny, both delivering ten days early.

The Avery baby comes out first, a girl, at 3:01 a.m., sixteen hours into labor, and next door, Brittany's baby emerges at 4:15. They are moved up to a special room, decorated by a staff of nurses who went crazy with balloons and crepe paper. Sometime around sun up, I'm told Avery's baby is named Paris Brittany Johnson and Brittany's baby is named Paris Avery Johnson (which might be the stupidest part of all this, but I don't say this aloud). Both babies are adorable and I hold them, one in each arm, and make the picture Jill takes of us the cover photo on my phone. I'm not inhuman; tears form just as the picture's snapped. I also take minor joy in seeing Max, who has gotten a free pass up to this point, ghostly with terror, babies ready to cry and poop and combine the two until he'll wishes he was a virgin again, not getting dates, not thinking anyone would ever like him. I think back to that Max and wonder which I'd prefer now, the boy who didn't think he'd ever be loved or the terrified still-boy who will become a man years before I ever did.

Night comes and it's time for Grandma, Grandpa, and Grandpa to go home. We drop Jesse off—he makes three obvious allusions to our guest room on the five-minute drive—and I get Jill to bed, her preparations for the babies' arrival overwhelming her, so much so she finally shuts up about how much she loves the name Paris. I need to sleep, too—two days from now will mark the end of sleep for all of us.

Before I go to bed, I climb up to the attic and dig out our high school yearbooks. I thumb through senior year first, when Jill and I dated. Jill was in drama, several candids of her in costumes spread throughout. Aside from my senior photo, there's only one shot of me, black glare paint under my eyes after losing the homecoming game. Next I crack my junior yearbook and flip to Lanette Mikowski, my girlfriend of two years at that point, the girl I thought would be Jill, especially when I got Lanette pregnant. The moment she told me, I proposed, Lanette accepted, and we were in heaven. But her parents forbade it. They wanted nothing to do with me or our baby. Two days later, they sent Lanette to Wisconsin to live with cousins and have the baby, which she would give up for adoption, then come home and not come near me again. My parents tried to stand up for me, but it didn't matter. Lanette had a miscarriage in her first trimester, but stayed in Wisconsin and I have no idea, today, what she does now. The September after she left, Jill sat next to me in civics class and that was that.

Every day since, I've thought of Lanette and that baby, how we felt the two glorious hours after I proposed, before we told her parents and they kicked me out of their house. Had Lanette stayed, maybe she wouldn't have had that miscarriage. Maybe we'd still be together, a different daughter or son in my life, maybe more kids, maybe not, me happy as I am now, never thinking twice about Jill, just another pretty girl I knew from school.

Ever since Max broke down and told me what he had done, I've been picturing Lanette and Jill together in my current house, two loving wives, nobody thinking it odd, everyone happy. I picture another son—a boy two years older than Max with my nose and Lanette's eyes—growing up as Max's brother, inseparable. I picture barbecues, three-way catch in the yard, me teaching them every path to manhood, to happiness.

And this is why I'll cherish these two baby girls of Max's, why I accept their moms, and why my son, stupid and scared and exhausted, will get everything he needs, will get more than he needs, and can stay in my house with his family as long as he wants, after I die, after Jill dies, this home his and theirs for all times.

# SALTED CARMEL PRETZEL

When I returned from the restroom, Salvator had switched places with the server. Two tables away, my husband scribbled orders onto a pad, while Kitty, recent waitress, sucked Salvator's straw, asked me what'd taken so long.

"My stomach," I said. "How's that shake?"

"Never ordered this before. You'd like it."

Salvator refilled water, cleared plates, boxed my leftovers. He brought the bill, a smiley face under the total that looked like a smirking baby. Kitty's apron snugged his waist, her blouse's buttons barely hanging on. I left two dollars, less than twenty percent. Salvator'd been stuck on fifteen forever. A bit of karma.

Kitty had Salvator's keys and knew where to find our Outback. She drove, following the exact way Salvator liked, using side streets, avoiding lights. He'd complained once that I loved the worst routes, hitting the reds like slalom gates. I never drove with him in the car again.

At home, Kitty fled upstairs and turned on the shower. I checked email and ate my tuna melt and pickle. When Kitty took forever to come downstairs, I went to bed, trying pajamas I'd never worn, their tags still attached. I watched TV until Kitty appeared, nude and smelling like gin, a towel around her head. She pulled on a pair of Salvator's running shorts and picked up his book from the nightstand, opening to the dog-eared page. She started reading, the book resting on her chest.

I turned over, Kitty's lamp fighting through my eyelids. I had work in the morning, my last shift until the weekend. I dozed until Kitty poked my shoulder. She pointed to a short paragraph, saying, "I did not see that coming."

"Of course you didn't," I said. I already knew what she would want from me next.

# THE MEAT SWEATS

It's 3 a.m. and I have the meat sweats real bad. I've been driving around since midnight because I can't go home, and in the suburbs, there's nowhere to go. I've done fifteen laps around the town and am thinking of getting a room, a place to shower, rest, regroup before facing Evelyn. If she sees me like this, we're through. If I don't get home in a couple of hours, it won't take her long to guess where I've been, anyway. And how I must reek. Either way, I'm cooked, and that's if the sweats don't get me first. Nothing would surprise me.

Then a coyote starts jogging alongside my car and I'm surprised. I've seen this coyote before, standing beside the "Welcome to Belmont!" sign at the outskirts of town, staring at me as I passed. This coyote has just one eye and, at fifteen m.p.h., keeps pace. I accelerate to twenty and he doesn't lose a step, not until I reach twenty-five. Then I catch a bad break: train. I stop and the coyote catches up. Fuck me if it doesn't leap onto the top of my car. Its head dips down to my window and I hear his growl through the glass. I put my car in reverse, spin around, vaulting the coyote onto the hood. I drive, the coyote staring in at me, its legs splayed, trying hold on and burst through the windshield at the same time. I slam on my brakes and it lunges forward, then

130

slips off on the passenger side. The tiny spider web in the windshield is one more thing I'll have to explain.

The last time I had the meat sweats, Evie nursed me back. She didn't preach while I was gorging myself on pork steaks, four full slabs in ten minutes. She didn't say a word while she held my hair back at the toilet, my temperature 103 and rising. While the EMTs pumped my stomach, she didn't rub it in, just held an icepack to my brow. When I was released two days later, she said she'd thrown out the bacon, two tubes of hamburger, the stack of sirloins in the freezer, a rotisserie chicken from Meijer, even the bacon bits from the cabinet. She said she'd be done with me if I ever put her through that again. I promised she was more important to me than meat, and that we'd grow old together. She believed me and I believed me, too.

At 4 a.m., cops pull me over. I've been swerving, half from nodding off, half from the sweats. I know they won't believe I'm not drunk, but I have the meat sweats and I'm trying to come down before I go home. This officer, Officer Lucido, isn't listening. His partner, a big guy who looks like he's known some sweats himself, stands idly by. Lucido thinks I've done a two-liter of blow and makes me walk the line on the side of the road. I stay straight, dizzy but in control, mosquitos buzzing my ear, fireflies dotting the bordering soy field. I wonder if the coyote's still tracking me, wounded but starving, me giving off this scent. The cops let me go, but not before the big one, Officer Joseph, hands me a brochure he fetched from their cruiser. The brochure is titled *The Meat Sweats* and there's a picture of a grieving widow at a coffin, flanked by two orphaned children, a boy and a girl.

When Evie was just eighteen, I introduced her to things she only thought she knew. She's from St. Louis, was a freshman at

UMKC, and granted that Chicagoans knew hot dogs and pizza, but pork ribs? Missourians had us there, their dry rubs and masterpieces and whatnot. I invited her to my apartment, where I kept a little hibachi on the balcony. While the coals fired orange, I dusted the raw pork with cayenne then laid the meat on the grid, an inch above the heat. She didn't intervene until I flipped the meat and used a paintbrush to douse the sizzling side with sauce. She told me I was ruining it, grabbing my arm. She swore that ribs should be dry, that sauce is put on at the table. I insisted she be patient—this was our fourth date—and she fidgeted but complied. I flipped and brushed two dozen times, layer after layer of sauce caramelizing into a crust. As soon as Evie bit down, I had her. At 105 pounds, she demanded seconds, thirds, fourths, until we were out of meat. From there, I dragged Evie down and I still owe her for that. She's found the will to walk away, two years now since her last sweats. I only wish I had her strength.

I pull into the driveway, sending the mailbox over my hood like the persistent coyote. Our bedroom light goes on and Evie greets me at the door in her robe. I'd stopped at Denny's to wash, but instead ordered their barbecue burger, rare, with onion rings and a Cherry Coke. I ask Evie to come with me and she follows. Outside, I drop my hibachi, the Kingsford, the lighter fluid, and my tongs into the trash receptacle by the garage. I turn to tell Evie I'm done, that I've relapsed but am D-O-N-E done, but she's gone. I expect to find her inside packing, maybe crying, but instead, she's rifling through the trash. Inside a grocery bag, inside a Styrofoam container, a dozen gnawed bones mingled with some coleslaw and a wad of used wet wipes. She drops the mess onto the floor and tells me she loves me. I tell her the same, pulling her against me, perspiration glistening her forehead, shining like gristle on the fifth flip.

# MEMORARE FOR THE DING DONG

When I remember the Ding Dong, I remember a girl. This girl and I were young, still in college, said, "I love you" too soon, good practice, but otherwise, words to fill the air. She hailed from Pennsylvania, was distinctly proud of being not Midwestern, and said "forest" like "farrest." She also knew "Ding Dongs" as "King Dons." I didn't believe her, that there were two names for the same thing, and without anyone to ask or the Internet around yet to check, I told her to have her parents send some in the mail.

Weeks later, we passed the Hostess display at the White Hen and I asked her if the King Dons ever came. She said no, smiling, and after I prodded her all the way back to her apartment about why not, she told me her father refused, that when she asked him, he said it was ridiculous, a waste of his time and hers. She agreed. "Did you really think my dad was going to drive to a store, buy a package of donuts, drive to a post office, and mail it to us, just to settle a bet? He's a doctor, you realize. He has a practice." I played it off as her having made it all up: Ding Dongs were Ding Dongs in Chicago, Pittsburgh, Philadelphia, and Paris, and King Don was the name of the Ding Dong mascot with the crown and scepter, friend to Twinkie the Kid, Captain Cupcake, and Fruit Pie the

Magician. Today, I recognize this as the beginning of the end, but back then, my feelings were just hurt.

That winter, over semester break, I traveled east with this girl, stayed in her house, met the honorable Dr. and Mrs. That's-Ridiculous, and on a trip to a drug store, saw the King Dons on the shelf, right there between the Ho Hos and Sno Balls. She elbowed me in the side and bought me a pack, but I didn't eat them. I wanted to take them home and show my family, people who would appreciate the humor of the other name as much as I did. They were good-humored people, and any one of them would have mailed anything to me I asked, whether it was to prove a point to someone, for a laugh, or to give them something to do. They would have driven a packet of mayonnaise down to my dorm at a moment's notice, just for an excuse to take me to dinner and check the oil in the Suburban. When this Pennsylvania girl and I left her parents' to drive back to school, I forgot the King Dons in the room where I'd slept, but it didn't matter. On the drive across the state, we decided to break it off. We would graduate that spring and if we weren't planning a wedding—and we weren't—there was no point. We drove the last eight hours listening to mix tapes, and when we got to her apartment, I picked up my toothbrush and never talked to her again.

When Hostess went under that year and everyone was crying the death of the Twinkie, I took my daughters to the Kroger and emptied the shelves of Ding Dongs, eight boxes of twelve, seven two-packs, plus some Ho Hos because they were close enough. We all ate one Ding Dong in the parking lot and I told them about some states calling them King Dons. They didn't believe me, either, and for some reason, I pointed out that these Ding Dongs were the last in existence. My youngest, four years old, started to cry. She'd never lost a grandparent or even a goldfish, and before then, may never have tasted a Ding Dong, either. But she was hysterical. My older girl, six, started crying, and then I started to cry, too, all of us in the van, at a stoplight, crying over Ding Dongs, dozens of Ding Dongs right there with us in the car. The light turned green and I didn't move, cars behind me honking their horns, and I reached into the open box on the seat and offered my girls another. "No, Daddy," my youngest said, pushing my hand away. "These need to last us the rest of our lives."

# ACKNOWLEDGMENTS

Thank you to my family, Karen, Ernie, Keats, and Salami. What I do is hard and you both endure it and help me thrive.

Thank you also to my family back in Chicago. Since I grew up Polish and Catholic, there's too many people to name, but I am lucky they've allowed me to do what I do, put me down this path.

I would also like to thank the following editors for accepting these stories in their journals: David Bowen, Casey Bye, David Carkeet, Jamez Chang, Dave Clapper, Heather Cox, Okla Elliott, Tagert Ellis, Matthew Fogarty, Jon Fullmer, Scott Garson, Tyler Gobble, Michael Griffith, Kirby Johnson, Todd Kaneko, Owen King, Tara Laskowski, George Looney, Amanda Marbais, John McNally, Richard Newman, Phong Nguyen, Don Peteroy, Todd Pierce, Adam Pieroni, Jennifer Pieroni, Nancy Stebbins, Steve Tartaglione, Jo Van Arkel, Brandi Wells, Jacob White, Lex Williford; a special mention goes out to the late Jeanne Leiby, whose editorial expertise and friendship I am particularly grateful for and miss.

Thanks to all of my teachers, colleagues, and friends at Bowling Green, *Mid-American Review*, Dzanc Books, the University of Illinois, Bowling Green, Moon City Press, and Missouri State, who are too numerous to name here, but without whom I could never have created this project.

I am especially grateful to everyone at Curbside Splendor for again giving me this opportunity and for showcasing my work. I am eternally grateful to Naomi Huffman, Alban Fischer, Ryan W. Bradley, Peter Jurmu, and Victor David Giron for all they did, do, have done, and will continue to do for me as a writer.

I am most grateful, however, to Jacob Knabb, as most of this is his doing.

Some of the stories in this collection appear or are forthcoming in various venues, often in slightly different forms and under slightly different titles. They are as follows:

*Counterexample Poetics*: "We Were Young"
*The Cincinnati Review*: "Hot Lettuce"
*Faultline*: "Marrow"
*The Florida Review*: "Thin Air"
*Ghost Ocean*: "High Treason"
*Green Mountains Review*: "The Last Time We Had Intercourse"
*Hayden's Ferry Review*: "Night of the Scallop"
*Hobart*: "All Out"
*Knee-Jerk*: "Man of the Year"
*Lake Effect*: "A Change of Heart"
*Mayday Magazine*: "Home"
*Natural Bridge*: "The Old Country"

*NANO Fiction*: "Salted Carmel Pretzel"

*NOÖ Journal*: "Kulkulkan"

*Pleiades*: "Opal Forever"

*Quick Fiction*: "Instead of Getting Married"

*Requited*: "Milo Himes"

*River Styx*: "Bullfighting"

*SmokeLong Quarterly*: "LAX," "The Meat Sweats," and "Pregnant
    With Peanut Butter"

*Sundog: The Southeast Review*: "Shelf Life"

*Wigleaf*: "The Plum Tree"

*Yemassee*: "Memorare for the Ding Dong"

"When the Heroes Came to Town" appears in the anthology
*Who Can Save Us Now?: Brand-New Superheroes and Their
Amazing (Short) Stories.*

"Plagues of Egypt" appears in the anthology *Snapshots: A One
Hundred Word Anthology.*

"Pregnant With Peanut Butter" is reprinted in *SmokeLong
Quarterly: The Best of the First Ten Years, 2003-2013.*

MICHAEL CZYZNIEJEWSKI is the author of two previous collections, *Elephants in Our Bedroom: Stories* (Dzanc Books, 2009) and *Chicago Stories: 40 Dramatic Fictions* (Curbside Splendor, 2012). He currently serves as an assistant professor at Missouri State University, where he edits *Moon City Review* and serves as the managing editor for Moon City Press. In 2010, he received a fellowship in fiction from the National Endowment for the Arts. He lives in Springfield, Missouri, with his family.

## DOES NOT LOVE
### A novel by James Tadd Adcox

*"... Adcox is a writer who knows how to make the reader believe the impossible, in his capable hands, is always possible, and the ordinary, in his elegant words, is truly extraordinary."*
—**Roxane Gay,** author of *Bad Feminist* and *An Untamed State*

Set in an archly comedic alternate reality version of Indianapolis that is completely overrun by Big Pharma, James Tadd Adcox's debut novel chronicles Robert and Viola's attempts to overcome loss through the miracles of modern pharmaceuticals. Viola falls out of love following her body's third spontaneous abortion, while her husband Robert becomes enmeshed in an elaborate conspiracy designed to look like a drug study.

## LET GO AND GO ON AND ON
### A novel by Tim Kinsella

*"I give Kinsella a five-thousand-star review for launching me deep into an alternate universe somewhere between fiction of the most intimate and biography of the most compelling. It's like ... a pitch-perfect fine-flowing bellow, the sound of celestial molasses."* —**Devendra Banhart**

In *Let Go and Go On and On*, the story of obscure actress Laurie Bird is told in a second-person narrative, blurring what little is known of her actual biography with her roles as a drifter in *Two Lane Blacktop*, a champion's wife in *Cockfighter*, and an aging rock star's Hollywood girlfriend in *Annie Hall*. Kinsella explores our endless fascination with the Hollywood machine and the weirdness that is celebrity culture.

## CRAZY HORSE'S GIRLFRIEND
### A novel by Erika T. Wurth

"Crazy Horse's Girlfriend *is gritty and tough and sad beyond measure; but it also contains startling, heartfelt moments of hope and love. In my opinion, a writer can't do much better than that.*" **—Donald Ray Pollock,** author of *Knockemstiff* and *Donnybrook*

Margaritte is a sharp-tongued, drug-dealing, sixteen-year-old Native American floundering in a Colorado town crippled by poverty, unemployment, and drug abuse. She hates the burnout, futureless kids surrounding her, and dreams that she and her unreliable new boyfriend can move far beyond the bright lights of Denver that float on the horizon before the daily suffocation of teen pregnancy eats her alive.

## THE OLD NEIGHBORHOOD
### A novel by Bill Hillmann

*"A raucous but soulful account of growing up on the mean streets of Chicago, and the choices kids are forced to make on a daily basis. This cool, incendiary rites of passage novel is the real deal."*
**—Irvine Welsh,** author of *Trainspotting*

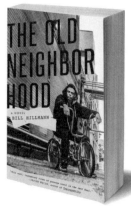

*The Old Neighborhood* is the story of teenager Joe Walsh, the youngest in a large, mixed-race family living in Chicago. After Joe witnesses his older brother commit a gangland murder, his friends and family drag him down into a pit of violence that reaches a bloody impasse when his elder sister begins dating a rival gang member. *The Old Neighborhood* is both a brutal tale of growing up tough in a mean city and a beautiful harkening to the heartbreak of youth.